The Book of Poison

Other story collections published by Evertype

The Book of Poison (Panu Petteri Höglund & S. Albert Kivinen,
tr. Colin Parmer & Tino Warinowski 2014)

The Partisan and other Stories (Gabriel Rosenstock,
tr. Mícheál Ó hAodha & Gabriel Rosenstock 2014)

Neighbours: Stories in Mennonite Low German and English
Nohbasch: Jeschichte in Plautdietsch und Englisch
(Jack Thiessen 2014)

The Burning Woman and other stories (Frank Roger 2012)

The Book of Poison

Stories inspired by H. P. Lovecraft

Four stories by
Panu Petteri Höglund

One story by
S. Albert Kivinen

Illustrated by
Mathew Staunton

evertype
2014

Published by Evertype, Cnoc Sceichín, Leac an Anfa, Cathair na Mart, Co. Mhaigh Eo, Éire. *www.evertype.com*.

A catalogue record for this book is available from the British Library.

ISBN-10 1-78201-058-0
ISBN-13 978-1-78201-058-6

Edited by Mathew Staunton and Michael Everson.

Typeset in Caslon and Caslon Antique by Michael Everson.

Illustrations: Mathew Staunton.

Cover: Michael Everson.
    Photograph by Andrejs Pidjass, Riga, *nejron.livejournal.com*.
    Photograph of Panu by Ruth Gaughan, London.
    www.magpiephotographic.com.
    Photograph of S. Albert by Sami Syrjämäki, Helsinki.

Printed by LightningSource.

Contents

Preface
to the Irish-Language Edition

Although I have had an interest in, and a thirst for, all kinds of prose, including horror stories, ever since I started reading, I had never heard of Lovecraft, nor of the Cthulhu mythos, until my university days, when Finnish writers of the genre started writing stories in the style of Lovecraft in an attempt to place the "Great Old Ones", the gods and monsters dreamed up by him, into a Finnish geographical and cultural context. Like Lovecraft himself, they tried their best to blur the boundaries between fact and fiction by putting in false references to historical events and places they knew.

S. Albert Kivinen was the pioneer of this Lovecraftianism in Finland. He spent many years lecturing on philosophical theories in Helsinki University, and his research focuses mostly on Ontology. He has a great fondness for English philosophers, such as Bertrand Russell, G.E. Moore, and C.D. Broad. Though a sceptic, a rationalist, and a materialist, he had always taken an interest in things otherworldly—superstition, sorcery, the occult and the like—as questions of philosophical and epistemological interest. If such things as ghosts, vampires, or the Loch Ness Monster really did exist, what kind of evidence and reasoning would be necessary to satisfactorily prove it? That's just one example of the kind of problems Kivinen reflected upon and took seriously. The students attending his lectures were never bored, and have many amusing anecdotes to tell about this extraordinary man.

Kivinen's pioneering efforts to make Lovecraft available to Finnish readers included his short story *Keskiyön Mato Ikaalisissa* ('The Midnight Worm in Ikaalinen'). Nowadays it is a minor classic in its genre, and in Finland it is read by everyone who enjoys Lovecraft's style. The story is set in the place where the writer himself was born and includes references to Finnish history: the civil war between the Reds and the Whites in 1918, for example, or the Swedish regency government under Finnish politician Gustaf Adolf Reuterholm at the end of the seventeenth century. The part played by Providence in the geography of "Lovecraft country" in the States could be said to be played by Ikaalinen in the "Cthulhuist" geography of Finland today, thanks to the impact of Kivinen's story on the genre there.

Kivinen's story came out in print for the first time in the magazine *Portti Science Fiction* in 1987, in a special edition dedicated to Lovecraft. The author republished it in 1990 in his book *Merkilliset kirjoitukset: Novelleja, artikkeleita, filosofiaa* ('*The Remarkable*

Scriptures: Short Stories, Articles, Philosophy'). This was an anthology of texts by Kivinen himself, published by Pirkanmaan Kirjapaino ja Lehtikustannus. It was the fourth volume in the series *Atlantis-kirjasto*, or "The Library of Atlantis" and, as I understand it, the other volumes came from the pens of people who really believed in this supernatural world. His third publication came hot on the heels of that one. Between 1980 and 1992 the Finnish Astronomical Society, URSA, published science fiction in Finnish, such as the works of Robert A. Heinlein, Orson Scott Card, and Clifford D. Simak, as well as collections of short stories by Finnish writers. In 1991, Raimo Nikkonen edited such an anthology of stories under the title *Keskiyön Mato Ikaalisissa*, taken from Kivinen's short story. It was upon reading this collection that I myself became acquainted with Kivinen's work.

At that time, in the early nineties, I was getting my first taste of the Irish language. The Irish speakers I knew were complaining that there was not enough reading material available in the language, and so I resolved to provide this kind of subject matter as soon as I had learnt the language sufficiently well. Part of that dream involved translating the story of the serpent in Ikaalinen which had so inspired us in Finland at the time, and I am proud that I was able to introduce it to Irish-language readers in Evertype's 2012 publication *An Leabhar Nimhe*, together with stories of that same ilk written by myself.

Panu Petteri Höglund,
Turku, Halloween 2012

Editors' Note

The editor and the publisher of this English-language edition of Panu Petteri Höglund's Lovecraftian stories, including the first English translation of S. Albert Kivinen's *Keskiyön Mato Ikaalisissa*, are proud to make the work of these Finnish authors available to a wider audience. We are grateful to Panu and to S. Albert Kivinen for agreeing to the translations, and would like to thank the two translators, Colin Parmar (Irish to English) and Tino Warinowski, (Finnish to English) for their excellent work.

Mathew Staunton
Michael Everson
Spring Equinox 2014

Cuitiliú

It is difficult to find any references to Cuitiliú in Irish literature. But that is not to be wondered at. Although the monks of ancient Ireland were happy enough to accept the Fenian Cycle and the Ulster Cycle as a pastime, they were not so welcoming towards the Cuitiliú Cycle. They had orders from God or from the Church to wipe out Paganism and diabolical practices throughout Ireland, as far as possible, and if Cuitiliúism wasn't considered diabolical practice, I don't know what would be. A tree is known by its fruit, and if the monks ever saw the terrible, poisonous fruits that grew on the tree of Cuitiliú, it would be small wonder that they didn't tear up every last root of that tree to throw on the bonfire.

Even so, it was natural that remnants of Cuitiliúism should survive here and there, even on the Island of Saints and Scholars. Amhlaoibh Ó Súilleabháin, in Callan, County Kilkenny, knew about it when he was writing his Diary, shortly before the Great Famine. As

1

we know, two important editions of this Diary were printed, the comprehensive McGrath edition and the selections put together by Tomás de Bhaldraithe. Both of them overlooked one manuscript which belonged, beyond a shadow of doubt, to the Diary, as it was written in Ó Súilleabháin's own hand. That said, it is well to remember that the diarist's handwriting clearly reveals his fear and panic, which is understandable enough given the content of the manuscript. Sometimes it is difficult to make sense of what he is saying, at other times it is hard to give it credence.

Basically, what happened is that Ó Súilleabháin and his friend, "Professor Physick" (that is, a medical doctor) Patrick Keeting, heard talk of "strange and wanton heathen rites" about the place known as Devil's Cliff. This manuscript is the only document in which the place is mentioned at all, as no other source makes any reference to Devil's Cliff. It seems that Ó Súilleabháin refrained from citing the real name of the location where these events took place as he preferred them not to be remembered by anyone. The only thing that can be said with some certainty is that the place is situated in County Kilkenny, far from any other human habitation.

When Ó Súilleabháin and the Professor came to the place, the first thing they saw was a man's head placed over the main gate of the village. The flesh had not yet fallen away from the skull completely, but there were nonetheless flies flying in and out of the eye sockets and a hollow droning sound could be heard from within. The two men had seen many horrors

before that, but they now felt a shiver of fear running through them and they had to take a pause to vomit that morning's breakfast onto the roadside.

Things only got worse when Ó Súilleabháin and the Professor went through the gate, for the place was littered with the remains of the great dying. Human bones and skulls were strewn willy-nilly about the place and used as a raw material. For the houses were adorned with them; and as well as that, bones roughly fashioned into tools could be seen lying about here and there. It was clear that these ghastly implements were not the work of trained craftsmen, but rather it seemed that someone of little skill had sought to turn the nearest bone to the task at hand, casting it aside once it had served its purpose, without a thought for the next occasion in which he might need such a tool again.

There was no doubt about it: people were killing and eating each other in this place. Ó Súilleabháin and the Professor knew full well that such a thing could happen if people had not enough food to eat. The strange thing about Devil's Cliff was that hunger was certainly not to blame for this cannibalistic epidemic. In fact it had been a long time since anyone had even attempted to harvest crops or milk or slaughter the cattle for food. The cows were left to wander about the place, some of them had gone feral, and some had died for want of care and attention.

At first Ó Súilleabháin and the Professor thought that there was no one left alive at Devil's Cliff, but in the end they met a handful of people, *more alike unto unreasoning beasts or black devils in their countenance and*

4

manners than human beings created by God, according to Ó Súilleabháin's own description of them in his manuscript. They were unable to put together an intelligible sentence in any language. One of them was laughing hysterically and trying to indicate to the Professor that he wanted to speak to him, but little sense could be made of the gibberish he came out with.

Ó Súilleabháin did his best to write down the stumps of speech he and the Professor heard from the poor fellow. The word he uttered the most was "Cuitiliú", and as well as that he spoke of "Cú-tú-gá" and "Sadogooa". Furthermore, he went on about the "Great Old Ones", or the "Great Elders", who were "asleep, awaiting their turn". "They will eat us," claimed the madman, "and 'tis a good thing, for happy is he who is eaten first!" The Professor could not but utter "By God!", whereupon the survivor grew angry. "No God," he said, "no God but Cuitiliú, and Cuitiliú will come to us to eat us, and happy is he who is eaten first! The Great Elders are older than Christ! They are older than the God of the Christians!" Then he began speaking in a language neither the Professor nor Ó Súilleabháin understood, although they could speak both Latin and French as well as Irish and English. Ó Súilleabháin noted down "Cuitiliú fa-tagh-an" from the mouth of the lunatic, and "Eádh Eádh Satógua".

Shortly after that, the English authorities came to Devil's Cliff to wipe out the "strange heathen rites". The whole village was burnt to the ground and the bones were buried in the same spot. As for the people who were left alive, the highest-ranking English officer decided to put them to death right away. He accepted all responsibilities for this slaughter. Upon studying the behaviour of the remaining survivors, he had come to the conclusion that they could not be cured, and he also thought that it may have been a contagious disease that had reduced them to such a state. He said that he considered it preferable to protect society at large from the contagion, even if that entailed the killing of these people.

The Great Famine struck Ireland a few years after these events. If any trace of the heathen beliefs had persisted in the surrounding area, it vanished along with the people. Stray memories of the cannibalism associated with the Cuitiliú cult may have survived, but even so, people most likely attributed them to the horrors of the Famine. Those who heard occasional tales about the cannibals of Devil's Cliff thought that hunger had been the cause of such atrocities.

It is difficult to come across even these hazy recollections in the folklore archives. As for the Schools' Manuscript Collection, it is already a well-worn cliché that much of importance was left out of it because the old people were not willing to tell every kind of story to small children. It is the best we have in Irish, however. Old people avoided talking about Cuitiliúism, even if they knew about it. Anyone who did happen to let anything slip one day would often be much more taciturn the next day. This is what old folklore collector Seoirse Mac Cuarta wrote in a place called Mín na bPléasc:

Cuitiliú

Only a few people were still able to speak Irish in Mín na bPléasc at that time, but even so, I got to know an old man by the name of Joe Jimín Shéamuis Mhóir, or Seosamh Ó Gallchóir. Joe Jimín was extremely knowledgeable about the folklore of the local area, and was unstintingly generous in bestowing his wealth of stories on me as soon as he understood what I was searching for there. He knew a good many old Gaelic stories, always reciting his own version embellished with a wealth of local words and turns of phrase. As well as that, he also made obscure references to stories I had never heard from any other storyteller before or since, stories which even he only remembered faint echoes of. Once he spoke to me of some sort of being by the name of Cutló.

SMacC: Did the old folk have any stories about the end of the world, about how the world would all come to an end?

JJ: They had the poem, the poem about the End Times. Many people had it then. Tom Beag Thomáis Bháin over on the other side of An Cnocán Gorm had his version, he was a tailor, you know, a tailor who had a lot of the oral tradition, both old stories and poems, but then, Babaí Bhán had a different version, she had her own version. She was an old woman and rather strange, you know, she always had her own ways, and she grieving since the police killed her son, God bless the souls of the dead, she probably lost her senses from then on, bless the mark.

Even so, she had the oral tradition, and she telling tales to herself from time to time, and the people going past would often stop and listen to Babaí's stories. She was rather strange, indeed, but she was friendly too, she liked it when people showed an interest in her stories, perhaps it softened the pain after the death of her son. Well now, she had her own telling of the End Times, and it was a telling full of terrible things. I often heard her telling it, but though I heard, I never learned it, for if frightened me so much that I couldn't keep my mind on the words and I listening to her.

SMacC: What was so terrible about it?

JJ: She talked a lot about the monsters who took possession of the world awaiting Judgement Day, but at the end of the story the Son of God didn't return. He would never come again, that was what she would say. There would only be the monsters at the end of the world, and Cutló was the most powerful of them. Cutló was lying at the bottom of the sea, and he sort of dead, but at the same time he wasn't really dead but sleeping, and he waiting for the day he would rise again and trample the world under foot and eat the entire human race, or make people eat each other...

I was not able to find out much more about these horrors. Afterwards the well of hospitality suddenly dried up, for Joe Jimín was no longer willing to talk with me, since he had uttered aloud the fateful name of Cutló. The next time I went to see him, I was turned away, for the old man had fallen unexpectedly ill and, as if that were not bad enough, his family firmly believed that I had been the cause of the poor man's bout of bad health. They were of the opinion that I was drawing blood from some old wound and enquiring into things that did not concern me at all. In the end, I had to leave the place, and whenever the next person (a man of my acquaintance) arrived there to record old stories and traces of the Irish language from the old people, Joe Jimín had already died, and the local people had all become very inhospitable towards strangers. They tried to make out that the religious sectarianism of the North was the reason for their reluctance, but the collector nonetheless realized that this was nothing but an excuse they had hurriedly thought up."

Quite apart from that, nobody knows where Mín na bPléasc is. It is most likely a false name, like Devil's Cliff. Mac Cuarta died shortly after that, leaving his manuscripts to his friend Proinsias Ó Conluain, but it seems that Ó Conluain did not make much use of them since he himself was afraid of their contents.

—Translated from the Irish by Colin Parmar

The Call of the Stars

My name is Máirtín Mac Cuarta. I learned Irish from both my parents, although I was born and raised in Dublin. My father was one of the few native speakers of Tyrone Irish, and although he had little regard for the language revival movement, he was of the opinion that his children should hear and learn the language at home. It was part of our people's heritage, and he impressed on us that one should not squander one's own heritage. My mother, too, was from Ceathrú Thaidhg in the North Mayo Gaeltacht, where the language was widely spoken when she was a little girl, and she spoke her own dialect to me for as long as I can remember.

My father knew a lot of stories and oral tradition from his native area, since the handful of Irish speakers left there used to visit his family home in the evenings. Many folklore collectors and students evidently used to come and visit to chat or to write down his stories—stories no one else knew in those days. I must admit that my father was not always welcoming of these visitors, but he did his best to humour them since he was a polite and well-mannered man. At the same time, however, he was worried that the visitors would take an interest in his manuscripts, the ones his own grandfather had left to his descendants and which he kept hidden away in a drawer, wrapped in a black cover with a lock and chain around them. They were writings in Irish about the "ancestors", as far as I understood as a young man, and there was magic in them, as he explained to me one day. "University people don't understand magic," my father once said. "They would cause a lot of trouble for us all, and for themselves too, if they got a look at the writings of the 'ancestors'." When I asked him who these "ancestors" were, I didn't get much information out of him. They were not the old Gaelic poets, but a much older group of people. Indeed they were older than God Himself, my father whispered to me, a look of terror in his eyes.

We were not particularly devout or dogmatic Catholics, but we were regular mass-goers nonetheless. My father placed his hope in religion as a source of solace and courage in this vale of tears. At the same time, he tended to think that the otherworld wasn't nearly as simple as the Christian religion would have us believe. He had a firm belief in ghosts, fairies, and spirits and he would even conjecture and theorize to himself about all these supernatural beings. Could you be sure that God's angels were mightier than these hidden forces? According to his understanding of things, no, you could not. This saddened his heart, and that sadness never left him.

The Book of Poison

When I asked my father straight out about the content of the writings, he was not able to give a proper explanation. But he stressed particularly that they were "visions of this Arab—a man who was surely mad, for he would not be able to help losing his mind after what he had seen."

Initially I took this to mean that it was the Koran— or perhaps a corrupted Gaelic version of it. The literati of ancient Ireland knew a lot and most of the ancient poets were able to read Latin. The first thought that occurred to me, as soon as I was old enough to contemplate the manuscripts myself, was that one of the poets came across the first Latin translation of the Islamic holy scriptures and wrote a long poem or epic summarizing the contents of the book, according as he himself understood it. As we know, Christians of that era were very hostile towards other religions, and one of the old poets might naturally look down on the Koran as "crazed visions from Arabia". When I talked about this theory with my father, all he did was shake his head at first, but then he replied that Mohammed and Jesus had both been trying to lessen the terrible fear of the "ancestors" that had gripped the entire human race. The "ancestors" had no compassion, pity, or mercy for man, said my father; but, at the same time, it was clear that the human mind could not cope with the truth about them, outlandish as they were. That is why good, understanding, good-hearted men like Jesus and Mohammed appeared from time to time to relieve us with their stories about the God of Mercy. They were men who understood the bitter truth of the universe and tried to protect the rest of humanity from it. That's the conclusion my father had drawn from them and from the great religious teachers of the world: Jesus, Mohammed, the Buddha, Zoroaster— you name them.

I was taken aback when I heard that, for it was obviously heresy from start to finish, no matter what your religion. But, at the same time, I acknowledged a sort of gap or void inside me: perhaps my father was right. Perhaps great and terrible supernatural forces were at work in the universe and perhaps they were stronger than any God—and they were not offering solace or promising mercy to mankind.

Although, as I said, I wasn't too devout a Catholic, I was still enough of a Christian to find this thought unacceptable. Even so, it was hard not to think that this terrible heresy stood to reason in some way. When faced with the wide open space out there, with its stars, quasars, and black holes, anyone would struggle to believe in the Christian God. According to our beliefs, the wellbeing of mankind was God's greatest concern, but in such a vast universe it was difficult to accept that God, the creator of it all, would bother too much about our fate. If there were gods, and they were so concerned about us, they mustn't be very important gods.

The result of this personal crisis was that I started taking an interest in the religion of the Ancestors. As I understood it, the Ancestors lived on certain stars up in the sky. So they were part of our universe, unlike the Kingdom of God according to Christianity, which was located in the supernatural world of angels

13

and demons. If you wanted to have recourse to God, you had to believe in the whole system of dogmas for which there was no other proof than faith itself. The Ancestors, on the other hand, were firmly rooted in this world as mapped out by scientists. There is nothing else. You could accept everything you read about astronomy, chemistry, physics, and biology and you could still have faith in the Ancestors. That's the kind of gods they were.

My parents died suddenly. Nobody expected it. It was an accident, or so we thought at first, but it was no ordinary accident. They were found dead in the wreckage of their car, but there was nevertheless something odd about the whole affair. They hadn't hit another car, or at least the forensics team couldn't find the paint of that car on the debris. The truth is that the authorities had no idea what had crushed them like that. And in a way, you could say that it was no earthly thing that did it, but fate. My fate.

I was twenty-something at the time and trying to study a bit at university. As soon as my father was buried, I went looking for the Ancestor papers in the cupboard. It didn't take me long to break the lock and get the chain off the cover. Then I started reading the first manuscript.

I was right. The religion, if it was a religion, expounded in the writings about the "Ancestors" conformed to scientific understanding. Of course, a lot of it was described in a very obscure way, but even so, at its core lay the undeniable truth. I spent many a day reading these manuscripts and mulling over what was in them.

The Book of Poison

I found out about the "Arab" too. "Abadulthasairíd" was his name, or what the Irish made of it at least. They must have mangled it badly, for when I trawled the world's great encyclopaedias, from the Britannica to the unauthorized English translation of the Great Soviet Encyclopaedia, I didn't come across any learned person from the Golden Age of Islam with a name anything like it. Amongst the papers I found a long poem in Irish, in the style the traditional storytellers, based on "the book of the souls of the dead" (or perhaps "the book of the names of the dead", I wasn't sure, the two words are very similar in Irish) by Abadulthasairíd. It seems that whoever composed the story spoke fluent Latin, as did many of the teachers in the hedge-schools, and had read a Latin translation of the Arab's book. It was clear that it wasn't the Koran, but some other book altogether, a book which told of the fateful mysteries of land and sea, of heaven and Earth.

I started going for walks out in the open at nightfall, trying to get a glimpse of one of the stars that were the abodes of the Ancestors.

It is not a wholesome occupation to be going around trying to identify stars up in the sky if you live in one of today's big cities. One night, while I was trying to get a look at Orion—one of the most easily recognizable constellations, even despite the city lights— a gang of street hooligans started playing up on me, and it looked like they had every intention of giving me a good hiding and making off with my money. Then, I instinctively looked up, and the first thing I

saw was Orion. And the following words came to my lips in spite of myself:

"In the middle of the Belt is where Cóndram lives."

That was one of the most obscure lines in the lore of the Ancestors, but now it was clear to me. Cóndram—whoever he was—lived on the central star of Orion's Belt, Alnilam. I directed my gaze towards the star, and then I started babbling in a language I myself didn't understand:

> *Mtaq'agh gaq Khon'dorm agodach,*
> *Vrat'agh toq Khon'dorm balonach!*

And then that star lit up like another sun—a sun that shone only on me. I saw—no, it wasn't that I saw, rather I *sensed*—the light drawing up into a fireball that plummeted down onto me and penetrated me to the core. I could feel a new heat growing in my muscles, new blood running through my veins—and when I looked down at my hands, I saw them changing. My fingers were getting longer and my clothes were falling off me as this change came over me. My skin fell away to reveal the fresh, healthy segments of an enormous flea.

When I looked ahead, I noticed the terror in the eyes of the hooligans. Not only did I notice it, I derived enjoyment and pleasure from the looks on the boys' faces. I reached out my hand, if you could call it a hand, and, catching hold of one of them, I thrust one of my new-grown fingers into him. Oh, such bliss! Words can't describe it! When I drank in his blood, when I gave him the venom which dissolved his veins and nerves and muscles, I could taste each layer and membrane, each bone and each cell, and I had never had such a good feed while I was a human being! I could feel the green blood surging and boiling up in my arteries, and I realized that the same pleasure, the same strangeness, could be derived from every living person on the face of the earth. All I had to do, basically, was reach out my tentacle and thrust in my venom.

Whatever it was I now had in place of legs, they allowed me to run very fast. It didn't take me long to catch up with the other hooligans and to get a taste of them. When I had finished digesting them, I got hungry again. At first I was a bit worried, because I realized that the main problem with this new form I had taken on was that my appetite was only satisfied for a second, then I needed more human food. But then again, what was the problem? There were enough people to kill to keep me going for a good while. Five billion across the entire globe, and reproducing faster than I could eat them.

—Translated from the Irish by Colin Parmar

The Book of Poison

ack at the beginning of the nineties, when I was
just a student with little Irish and less money, I
published an announcement in *Anois*, a weekly
magazine that existed at that time, asking readers to
send me their old Irish-language books to help a poor,
stuttering learner from overseas. The kind and
generous Gaels did not belie their reputation, and I
received a good quantity of books from the magazine's readership, and without a doubt it was a great
help to me in improving my Irish. I received *An
Giorria san Aer* by Ger Ó Cíobháin, a Gaeltacht auto-
biography, the kind that it's best to read when you're
cosily tucked up under your blanket by the fire, as
well as *Rotha Mór an tSaoil* by Micí Mac Gabhann, the
most exciting and action-packed of the old Gaeltacht
autobiographies, and *Dialann Deoraí* by Dónall Mac
Amhlaigh, a long chronicle of migration in the fifties.
Although that was a long time ago and much has
happened since then, I believe that this first reading

material left its mark on my Irish to this day, and that is no bad thing at all.

On the other hand, however, one book arrived that I have not spoken about with any Irish speaker until now, because if I understand rightly, it is a quite extraordinary book. You could even say that it is a book that could alter the fate of the whole of humanity like no other could.

I received this book through the post, just like the other gifts people had sent me. The sender's name was nowhere to be found on the package, nor was there any letter enclosed with it—there was nothing but the book itself inside. It was a black book with no drawing or illustration of any kind on the cover, just the title itself, in bold gilt type:

AN CHUITILÍOCHT.

Well, it must have been a relatively recent publication. If it had been more antique, the title would more than likely have been spelt **An ċuiꞇiliꞇeaċꞇ**. But what was the *Cuitilíocht*? I had heard about the *Fiannaíocht* and the *Rúraíocht*—the Gaelic names for the Fenian Cycle and the Ulster Cycle respectively— and even the *Artúraíocht*, the Arthurian Cycle, but the *Cuitilíocht* was completely new to me. I had a look in Ó Dónaill and Dinneen, two of the main dictionaries of the Irish language, but to no avail—*Cuitilíocht* wasn't mentioned in them, nor any word or stem that resembled it.

When I started reading the book, I was expecting feats of valour and heroism after the fashion of the old Gaelic stories. Instead, I was surprised to find that

The Book of Poison

Cuitilíocht was a sort of occult knowledge. Here are a few examples of the kind of thing I came across in the book:

CUITILIÚ is the eldest of the Great Old Ones, and though he died, it was no permanent death that would not allow him to rise again, and He will return when the old stars are in the right place...

Study the surface of the water, Reader, and do not believe that mankind could know the beings and monsters who live in that cold, wet world below. In truth, since the beginning of time on the surface of the earth, there were tribes struggling to survive down there, tribes which only the oldest fishermen have heard vague references to, references they only dimly recall, and it is so much the better for their peace of mind...

When you enter one of those cities, you will see the farthest houses close to you and you will hardly recognize the nearest houses, so small shall they appear to you, and when you reach out your hand, you will think that it is inside where it is outside, and the very light will bend and curve...

This *Cuitilíocht* really was completely unlike the Irish myths in every way! And, to tell the truth, these stories would frighten you like nothing else. At that

23

time, I was living in a small, cramped flat in a student housing block, with a tree growing outside whose branches would rap on my window pane from time to time when the wind was getting up. Now, with these stories running through my mind, the tree seemed to take on a new and threatening appearance. When I looked up from my books, I would get a shock, for I thought for a second that I had seen some monster outside there watching me. As well as that, I had the impression that the day was renouncing its light before time, and I turned on the reading lamp above my bed. When the light from the lamp struck the page of the book, it started to shine or glow strangely, as if the paper were drinking in the energy from the light, holding it in for a second and then letting it out again. What kind of substance were the pages of that book made of? It was no ordinary paper, at any rate.

To cut a long story short, I almost went mad with terror while I was reading that bloody book. At the same time, I couldn't put it down. I used to take it with me everywhere and read a bit whenever I had a moment. People who knew me could see that I wasn't quite right anymore too. My Russian professor told me that I was as pale as death and asked me quite worriedly if I had leukaemia or yellow fever. When I told her that I was just frightened by what I was reading in Irish, she said that she had told me time and again that I was just wasting my time and effort trying to speak Irish, and that I should go back to Solzhenitsyn's tales about Stalin's labour camps, since I didn't find them nearly as scary as that Irish book. She was very scornful.

But she was right. After all, while I was studying German and Russian, I read every book I could lay my hands on about the horrors of the two great totalitarian systems, Communism and Nazism. You wouldn't think this world or the otherworld would hold any terror for me anymore, at least not in book form. Even so, there was some magic—or necromancy, perhaps—in the *Cuitilíocht* book that I couldn't ignore.

I hid the book somewhere where I wouldn't unwittingly catch a glimpse of it, and I tried my best to forget about *Cuitiliú* and *Cuitilíocht*. But I wasn't able to banish the book from my thoughts.

One day I was lost in thought, as was often the case. I wasn't paying any attention to what was going on around me, not a very sensible thing to do during rush-hour traffic, of course. I was almost hit by a car, but, by sheer good fortune, there was a policeman there who grabbed me at the last minute. He snatched me out of the path of the car before I even knew what was happening.

He was a middle-aged man with a full beard. I got a good telling off from him about how careless I had been with the traffic—I should look before crossing the road, and it was the custom to cross where there was a zebra crossing or traffic lights, by the way. What was I thinking about that was so interesting when I should have been dodging cars?

"A book," I said. "A book I was sent from Ireland. The author's name isn't on it, but it's full of strange horror stories."

The Book of Poison

You wouldn't think that a policeman would be into reading in a big way, but you would be wrong. When I mentioned the book to the man, he suddenly changed his tune.

"An anonymous book of horror stories, you say? From Ireland?"

"That's right," I said, "I'm learning Irish, you know, the language they spoke in Ireland before the English language came and took over. Irish people send me their old books to help me learn. Although native speakers of the language are only a small minority now, it's studied and used all over the island, including the North." I was often asked what on earth the Irish language is, and so I reeled off my well-worn explanation almost automatically.

The policeman only became even more curious when he learned that it was an Irish-language book. "I myself collect books, as a hobby, and horror stories are my favourite genre: Poe, Dunsany, Bram Stoker, all that kind of stuff. I don't speak a word of Irish myself, but I've heard that there's some interesting ancient literature in the language. I'm Sergei Susi, by the way," he said, holding out his right hand for me to shake.

I was quite glad that the policeman had turned so friendly, and I introduced myself. "I'm Panu Höglund," I said.

"Well, if it's no bother, I wouldn't mind taking a look at the book. Do you know where the Literary Café is? We could discuss the book there after I finish work."

Since that café was an old haunt of mine, I didn't hesitate to accept the appointment there. We decided to meet up in the café on the afternoon of the following day.

I was waiting for the policeman for half an hour, with the book in my bag. I got a cup of coffee and some kind of biscuit, and settled down to read that morning's newspaper, but in the end Sergei arrived. He greeted me, and we began to talk.

Sergei Susi wasn't his real name, but it came to light that that was the name most of his acquaintances knew him by. He had published his writings in the literary magazine under that name. He wasn't too fond of the name he was christened with, as it was simply one of the common Finnish names you would forget as soon as you heard it. Sergei Susi, on the other hand, that was a name that would stick in your head!

"You say you came across the name 'Cuitiliú' in the book."

"Yes. It's a name that has no connection with Irish mythology as far as I know. There's Bricriu—a sort of trouble-maker like the Norse Loki, if I'm not mistaken—but I've never come across Cuitiliú in any collection of folklore or in the standard versions of the mythology. So, do you know what 'Cuitiliú' means or what it refers to?"

"Well," said Sergei, "what I think is that it's a corrupted form of 'Cthulhu'."

"*Cthulhu*? What's that?"

"When I first heard of Cthulhu, I thought it was just some nonsense from a school of horror writers in the

United States. The first person to mention Cthulhu was Lovecraft, Howard Phillips Lovecraft..."

"It that his real surname?" I asked. "It sounds like the name of a porn shop."

The policeman laughed. "As far as I know it's his real surname. He was a loner with old-fashioned habits and ideas, and all the company he had was the ancient books he found in the family library. He even learned to use eighteenth-century English in his writings as he thought that was the true standard of the language."

"Well, it sounds like he was a bibliophile without equal."

"He certainly was. Now, as it happens, he would often refer to the 'Cthulhu mythos' in his writings, and the young writers who took an interest in his work would make references to the same thing. At first, when I was reading his books, I thought this myth was just an invention of Lovecraft. But then I met Joose-Alfred Kivelä, and I got a whole new understanding of it."

"Joose-Alfred Kivelä? Wait a minute... isn't he the professor of philosophy at Helsinki University who's interested in ontological issues?"

"The very same. He's not just an ontological philosopher, he's also Finland's leading expert on the Cthulhu mythos."

"And he thinks this mythos is more than just a story that Lovecraft made up?"

"Exactly. He did some research on the folklore of his own region and he came across a lot of things that couldn't be explained except in terms of the Cthulhu stories. He was the one who first got me searching for a book about Cthulhu. You know, Lovecraft made a lot of references to old books and manuscripts about Cthulhu, and the big question now is, did these books really exist at all, or were they only ever props for the writer's stories?"

"Did you ever find a copy of any of these books?"

"Well, have a look at this," said Sergei. He handed me a photocopy, a grey page with the following words on it:

"Eine kurze und konzise Abhandlung von ver-botenen, untersagten, fernländischen, überseeischen, merkwürdigen, ausserirdischen, ausserweltlichen, er-schrecklichen, unmenschlichen, todgeweihten, tod-bringenden, unterirdischen, unterseeischen, unge-heuren, weltenzerstörenden, ewigzerstörerischen, ewigkeitsüberdauernden, geheimgehaltenen, geheim-zuhaltenden, verheimlichten, verborgenen—" (and lot of other German adjectives) "—und gar *unaus-sprechlichen Kulten*".

That was the title of the book, and quite a hefty title it was too. To be honest, I standardized the German a bit for the benefit of those who speak the modern language—the original had "Culten" rather than "Kulten", and "erschrecklichen" was spelt "er-schröcklichen". The title was printed as a pyramid, with the two final words as the base of the pyramid.

"Well," I said, "that's the kind of title you'd see on a German book from the Baroque period."

"That's right," agreed Sergei. "It was a man by the name of Friedrich Wilhelm von Junzt who committed it to paper, but he had probably gone to meet his maker by the time it came into print for the first time, in 1839 in Dusseldorf. Joose-Alfred went in search of information about the writer, and he came to the conclusion that Junzt was only really republishing material from much older German sources. Joose-Alfred even thought that the language seemed much more ancient than you would expect to see in a nineteenth-century book. What about you, do you speak good German?"

I felt a little smile spreading across my lips when he asked me: "German studies is my main subject at university, and to tell the truth, I spoke fluent German before I even came to university."

"Excellent!" he said. "You should have a good long chat with Joose-Alfred, you're just the person he's looking for. He'll be coming to visit one of these days, and if I may, I'd like to introduce you to each other. But now, let's have a look at that book of yours. You did bring it, didn't you?"

"I certainly did," I replied. I plunged my right hand into my bag and took hold of the book. I handed it to him and he eagerly took it from my hands, just as you would imagine a man whose only interest in life was old books.

When he got hold of the book, he was astonished. He was trembling as he leafed through it here and there. When at last he spoke, his face was as pale as a corpse lying in a cold grave:

"You told me it was a book in Irish, from Ireland."

"I did indeed," I replied. "This is the book I was talking about. I couldn't have brought another one by mistake, as it's quite a distinctive book, and I've been keeping it hidden away in a special place until now."

"Well," said Sergei after a long pause, "if this is Irish, I didn't know it was a language so closely related to Finnish." He opened the book and showed me the pages. At first I thought it was Irish, but then the language slowly began to alter, and in the end it was Finnish. The size of the letters and the font didn't change, but one language replaced the other.

As for the Irish version, the text had adhered to the modern standard, and there was nothing in it that would hint at the author's dialect. In fact, when I read the first part of the book, I was surprised that there was no trace of any dialect in it—nor even the sort of Anglicisms you would see in the works of writers who had learnt Irish as a second language. Of course, the language was rich, full of turns of phrase from the language of the old Irish storytellers, but for the most part you would think it was a robot or a computer that wrote the book, rather than a human being.

And that's what the Finnish was like too. The writer paid close attention to the latest recommendations from the language planning centre. As the book was written, the words would show you no mercy whatsoever. This was the bitter truth, you would think, and there was no protective shield between you and that truth.

Just as I was examining the pages Sergei had put under my nose, we heard a man's voice saying in Finnish with a slight foreign accent:

"Oh, where did you get a book in my mother tongue?"

The Book of Poison

I looked up from the book to see a tall, stately black man standing next to me. He was obviously the one who had spoken. I was lost for words for a couple of seconds. Then I replied:

"Sorry, sir, I'm afraid you're mistaken. This book is in Finnish."

The man looked again at the book, and a look of disappointment came over him. "You're right," he said, "It is Finnish. But for a moment there, you know, I thought it was Amharic."

"So, you're from Ethiopia, then?" said Sergei.

"Yes, that's right, I'm Ethiopian," said the man in a deep voice in which a certain pride in his race could be detected, "I've been living here for five years now." He shrugged his shoulders. "Well, it's not important, but I could have sworn it was Amharic. We have our own alphabet, you know, and I was so sure that I recognized it." Then he said goodbye and left.

"Irish, Finnish, Amharic," I said. "Everyone sees whatever language they want to see in the book."

"I thought it was in Finnish," said Sergei, "and it was in Finnish. That man saw Amharic letters at first, but when we told him differently he changed his mind."

"I got it in the post," I remarked, "and since I was expecting an Irish book, I thought it was in Irish."

Now Sergei noticed the strange material the pages were made of.

"This isn't normal paper," he said. In light of the miracle we had just witnessed, that of the book changing language according to who was looking at it, I burst out laughing when I heard what Sergei had said. Perhaps I was so startled that I was getting hysterical. But then I got a grip on myself and spoke sensibly:

"No, indeed it isn't. It's as if the material absorbs the energy from the light for a minute, and then lets it out again after a while. Perhaps there's a scientific explanation for it."

Scientific explanation, my arse! I was clearly just trying to put my own mind at ease. If the different versions could be seen when the light was at different angles, maybe optics experts would be able to explain the phenomenon. Films of very fine material fastened tightly together, for example, each one printed with a version in another language, perhaps. But now, everyone was seeing the book in the language they were expecting to see, or in the language they were able to read.

And another thing, there was some sort of limitation associated with it, since I wasn't able to get the book back into Irish anymore. It was all in Finnish now and no other language, and that was that. So it was useless to me now as a resource for learning Irish, and when Sergei asked me to lend him the book, I was only too happy to let him have it. To be honest, you could say that I got disgusted with the book when it changed language, but that only increased Sergei's craving for it. Or perhaps it was the book that got a taste for Sergei?

"You can do whatever you like with the book," I said, "as it seems there's no longer any Irish in it anymore." I could see that Sergei had taken a real liking to the book, for he poured forth his gratitude on me from the bottom of his heart when he heard that I was willing to let him keep it.

After that, I studied hard at the Irish books I still had after giving away that mysterious one. Since my heart was really in the language at that time, as it still is, it didn't take me long to forget all about that strange book. One day, however, I received a letter from Sergei which was completely at odds with the level-headedness of the man I had once met:

Dear Panu,

Joose-Alfred came to visit me to read and discuss the book. He says that it is the Book of Poison, a book that was printed for the first time in the Nameless City, in a land that had long disappeared when the human race came of age. There are such books as Necronomicon or Unaussprechlichen Kulten which describe the mysteries of the gods and the beings who existed before mankind, but even so, they are only defective reworkings of this one. What we have now is the Original, the Book of Poison, that those other books are based on, and now Joose-Alfred and myself hope to take the poison out of the book as we get to work revealing all the mysteries...

He babbled away like that for page after page, but somehow, however enthusiastic Sergei had been when he penned the letter, this nonsense just bored me. To be honest, what I gathered from the whole long-drawn-out story was that it was just a wild goose chase and nothing good would come of his endeavours. At the same time, I instinctively sensed that Sergei was following his destiny now, and there was nothing I could do to stop him. I don't know why the letter inspired that kind of emotion in me, but it seemed like the most natural reaction in the world.

Some time later—two weeks, maybe—two police-men came to the door to ask me some questions. It seemed that Sergei and his friend Joose-Alfred Kivelä had disappeared. They had vanished without a trace, and since Sergei was one of their own, the police were very worried about the whole affair. At first, they made out as if they suspected me, but since I was very understanding, they quickly became more friendly. They took notice of what I said when I told them everything I knew.

Well, of course, if I had told the police about the book that changed language, they wouldn't believe a word I said. So the version of events they heard from me was that it was a Finnish book right from the start, an old book Sergei held in high regard. The police-men knew how keen their friend was on old books, and so they didn't bother asking too many questions about this one. I gave them the letter Sergei had written me, and then they took their leave. They never darkened my door again after that.

Sergei and Joose-Alfred were well-known figures amongst book lovers and science fiction enthusiasts in this country, and when they disappeared in such an incomprehensible way, all kinds of rumours and reports were going around. Luckily enough, no one ever found out about my connection with the case. Sergei knew everyone in Turku: policemen and criminals, students and professors. No one else apart from myself and the police knew who he got the book from. To tell the truth, many people thought it was quite a romantic death, the kind of death a book lover should die, if indeed it was a book that brought about his downfall.

As for the *Book of Poison* itself, it vanished together with the two men, and it was never heard of again after this strange episode.

—Translated from the Irish by Colin Parmar

The Midnight Worm in Ikaalinen

A short story in the style of Lovecraft by
S. Albert Kivinen

To H. P. Lovecraft *ad maiorem Cthulhus gloriam*

> O Rose, thou art sick!
> The invisible worm
> That flies in the night,
> In the howling storm,
>
> Has found out thy bed
> Of crimson joy,
> And his dark secret love
> Does thy life destroy.
>
> —William Blake

Chapter I

The Horror of Ruutinkari

Now that more than twenty years have passed since that mysterious explosion on the island of Ruutinkari in Ikaalinen, it is time to divulge the facts as I remember them. I will understand if you find my story unbelievable. Sometimes I doubt it myself. On the other hand, my recently deceased friend, H. Herbert Bladh, Adjunct Professor of Cryptochronology at the Åbo Akademi University, was personally involved in those events and, despite his numerous eccentricities, he was one of the sanest people I have ever known. I later discussed them with him but, contrary to what you might expect, I did not discuss them often, for they were events I would rather forget. If the hypotheses of my friend contain even a sliver of truth, many untold horrors may stalk humanity…

As some readers may well remember, the explosion on Ruutinkari in February 1965 provoked a number of wild rumours. A few newspapers even speculated that underground nuclear tests were being carried out in Finland, contrary to the provisions of the Paris Peace Treaty. It is said, though I cannot vouch for this, that some reporters received angry letters from the president, after which these speculations were promptly terminated.

I lived in the market town of Ikaalinen for a few years at the end of the fifties and got to know the area quite well. It was at that time—and still is—an ideal place to spend the summer. Located on a promontory far from any city, the market town is surrounded on three sides by lake Kyrösjärvi and divided in two, with *Kirkonkylä*, the "Old Church Village", bordering the market town and *Pitäjä*, the "Parish", an affluent rural area, on the opposite side of the lake. In summertime Ikaalinen really was idyllic. "Ikaalinen is the oldest, smallest, and most beautiful market town in Finland," the residents would say with pride. The buildings were, for the most part, old, single-storeyed, wooden houses, each with its own garden. You did not need to look far for possible excursions. The lakesides were largely untouched, owing to the fact that summer villas were not yet very common. After rowing for a short while you could disembark at Kaaresniemi or Puntunlahti, or if you fancied wider vistas and a bit of adventure, you could pitch a tent on one of numerous islands in the lake.

Among all of the islands, there was only one that was avoided by the locals: Ruutinkari. Located a few kilometres from the market town, it was, according to the folklore of the region, named after sergeant major (later lieutenant) J. J. Roth (1772–1839), who hailed from Ikaalinen and served with distinction in the Finnish War. Ruutinkari itself was nothing more than a rock with the ruins of a wooden house on top. Occasionally I suggested rowing out there, but the suggestion was always met with an awkward silence. Some of my friends said that we would be attacked by nesting seagulls. Others murmured, with no small degree of embarrassment, something about snakes having being found on the island. But no matter the explanation, the discussion was always promptly turned towards other matters.

Naturally, my curiosity was aroused by the fear surrounding Ruutinkari. I asked the locals what the ruined house had been. Had somebody lived there? Finally I received an answer from an elderly man: "It was that mad master, old Rolfwén," he said, before hastily changing the subject. A visit to the vicarage yielded more information: Master of Arts Göran Fredrik Rolfwén, born 1870, died 1926, married 1894 to Anna Elizabeth Grönberg, b. 1874. Moved to Helsinki 1897, divorced 1902.

What had this "mad master, old Rolfwén" done to make his very name taboo? I deduced from hints that he had ended his life in a mental hospital (Hatanpää, in the city of Tampere, to be precise). Mental illness was at the time a thing to be feared and never talked about, but this was hardly an adequate explanation. Although people refused to discuss the mental problems of their kin, and were even more tight-lipped about their own problems, the mad relatives of others were talked about with abandon. Why was Rolfwén an exception? And he without a single relative in Ikaalinen.

Gradually I began to feel that something mysterious and sinister was lurking under the calm, idyllic surface of Ikaalinen. Sometimes, as I sat in the large cool

rooms of those ornate wooden houses I shivered and strange thoughts crept into my mind: *no one would hear if...* if what? Life in Ikaalinen was placid and slightly monotonous, so that all local scandals were blown into cosmic proportions. Of course, it was true that there, as was the case elsewhere, family tragedies were kept hidden behind respectable facades. But there was something else here, some secret paralyzing horror which people were afraid to admit even to themselves. As autumn nights grew darker, Ruutinkari and its ruined house looked increasingly ominous. If a north wind was blowing, the parents hurried their children home, saying "That's a worm wind." Nobody dared to explain what a "worm wind" was. Did they believe that the wind somehow contained worms or their eggs? And why was the term applied to a north wind rather than a west wind? For there was a picturesque ridge west of the market town called Matomäki (Worm Hill). Why did the worm wind not blow from Matomäki? On one occasion an old man began to answer the question: "before old Rolfwén's time it did blow from Matomäki," but he quickly fell silent. A deathly pallor spread across the faces of the women present, and one of them suddenly started to recount the details of her trip to Tampere the week before in a loud voice and with undue precision, even though, as far as I could tell, she had already told the same story to the assembled group. On another occasion, a fisherman blurted out: "I too have a doe's bone in my net and, damn, there is a lot of fish..." but he, too, fell silent suddenly. Was a doe's bone a good luck talisman for fishermen? Was there magic here that outsiders were not to be made privy to? Either way, nobody was willing to tell me.

Once, in the late fifties, I hiked around the Kiviniemi cape equipped with my binoculars. This was quite close to Ruutinkari and I took advantage of the opportunity to study that ominous rock, and the abandoned building upon it. The house was in a truly shabby state: the roof had partially collapsed in, the door hung wide open, and all the windows were broken. A harsh autumn storm might cause the hovel to collapse altogether. A squabble of seagulls hovered in the breeze around the island, and I noticed something curious about them: *not one landed on the rock, not one took off from it, and not one flew over it*. It was as if they would have gladly made use of such an excellent nesting site, but were prevented from doing so by some invisible electric fence. As I had by now grown used to Ruutinkari being a forbidden topic of conversation in Ikaalinen, I kept this observation to myself.

Chapter II

The Riddle of the Folk Poems

The mysterious master Rolfwén had become an enigma which increasingly vexed my mind. What sunless secrets were connected with him that his shadow should becloud the otherwise charming market town? In my free time I strove to learn more, but the documents I found yielded almost no information. According to the registry of the Imperial Alexander University, Rolfwén matriculated in 1887 and graduated with a bachelor of arts degree in 1892. His subject combination was rather queer: he majored in both chemistry and oriental literature. He joined the Nation of Western Finland, but took little part in the Nation's activities. After a divorce, his ex-wife married a Swedish-speaking businessman and died at the end of the forties, surviving her husband by only a few years. They had children, two of whom were still alive, but they knew nothing of their mother's first husband. In fact they were surprised to hear of their mother's previous marriage at all. Rolfwén's relatives were of little use. A few cousins once removed were still living, but they too were unable to shed any light on the matter. The most informative answer came from an octogenarian lady: "*Ja, farbror*

The Midnight Worm in Ikaalinen

Göran, han var en mycket egendomligt karl!" ("Yes, Uncle Göran, he was a very strange chap!")

The summer of 1960 was the last I spent in Ikaalinen. A paper recycling drive was underway and I contributed a stack of newspapers. With a slight feeling of sadness I gazed at the printed material in the container. Some people had brought old books, which, in my mind, deserved preservation, and I salvaged a book of hours, printed in the late nineteenth century. It was by no means a bibliophilic treasure, but merited a better fate nonetheless. At home, I examined the book more closely. Folded inside was a sheet of paper, yellow with age and printed on both sides. It appeared to be an old broadside. On one side was a fragment of a poem describing how Finland was enriched by "deeds of the economic society, during the reign of good Gustaf". This suggested a publication date: the Economic Society of Finland was founded at the time of Gustaf IV Adolf in 1797, meaning that the poem must have been written a few years later around the year 1800. The poem on the other side gave credence to this hypothesis: it mocked the occult pastimes of Duke Karl and his "Grand Vizier" Reuterholm. As the caretaker government had ended in 1796, it was likely that poems mocking the defeated "Grand Vizier" were written during the subsequent years. The last part of the poem hinted that Reuterholm's knowledge and skills were nothing compared to the true arts of a seer. And then I received a shock, as if I had been bitten by a snake: *there was a mention of THE WORM WIND.*

In its entirety, the poem ran like this:

The Book of Poison

Reuterholmi, Ruotsin herra,
mitä tiiät, mies mokoma,
panet pöyät pomppimahan,
houkuttelet henkiäsi
Kaarle-herttuan keralla.
Pöyät pomppii, henget hourii,
vaan et löyä viisautta,
pnakotaitoja tavoita.
Saatkos Kutkan kalan suusta,
Satakuuan maan sisästä?
Etpäs manaa matotuulta,
kivirinkejä rakenna.
Lapsen tieto, naisen muisti,
ei oo NECRO *nyrkeissäsi,*
Apu allasi hajoa.

("Reuterholm, lord of Sweden,
what know you, poor man:
you make the table bounce,
entice your spirits
with duke Carl at your side.
Tables bounce, spirits moan,
but wisdom you shall not find,
nor reach *pnako*-skills.
Do you gain the Itch from the mouth of a
    fish,
Satakuua from beneath the ground.
No worm wind will you summon,
nor build circles of stone.
Child's wisdom, woman's memory,
no NECRO in your grasp,
Help crumbles beneath you.")

46

The Midnight Worm in Ikaalinen

I stared at the end of the poem without comprehending anything. What were the "pnako-skills" which Reuterholm was mocked for lacking? What was the "Itch (*kutka*) in the mouth of a fish"? Was "*Satakuua*" perhaps a printing error? Should it have read Sata*kunta*, a district in Western Finland? Building "circles of stone" would, it seemed, summon the "worm wind", but what was this "*NECRO*" that was not in "the grasp" of Reuterholm? Was it related to the dark arts of *necromancy*? Was the writer trying to express something that in more modern terminology would be rendered as "you can't handle it, the dark art of necromancy"? The last line was the most enigmatic of all: why did success require that help crumble beneath you?

My mind was awash with questions; not one had a reasonable answer. I spent almost the whole of that summer night walking the streets of Ikaalinen. I walked past the preparatory school to the laundry and stopped to look at the mysterious Matomäki looming in the distance a few kilometres away, whence the worm wind had blown before Rolfwén's time. What secrets were hidden on that ridge? Did it radiate a dark threat? Trees growing on the top of the ridge formed patterns reminiscent of prehistoric lizards... Preoccupied by these intense thoughts I turned right, walked along the side of the sports field to the old baths and from there to Rantopää, where again I could gaze upon the gloomy enigma: Ruutinkari, with its ruined house. Did Göran Rolfwén attempt to acquire "pnako-skills", whatever they might be? There was some mist on the lake, and on Ruutinkari it seemed

47

to condense into ghostly formations. And I could swear that *something was moving on the island...* I forced myself out of that dreamlike state. I needed to keep my wits about me, or who knew what I would start seeing.

I made a wide detour along an old road which, in a rather macabre fashion, was called "Devil's Alley", and returned along Rahkola lane to the market town. Was I becoming paranoid, or did curtains stir in one house after the other, with cold, discerning eyes following my movements? *Soon they would be upon me...* Rubbish, who would be upon me? Of course, the local busybodies kept an eye on passers-by from between their curtains, but they were all asleep now. On the other hand, did such a monotonous life not cause souls to develop strange yearnings and dreamy visions? Or perhaps I was experiencing an outbreak of something unknown and terrifying here? It must have been half past three when I got home, still troubled by these uneasy thoughts.

I spent the next ten days in Helsinki attempting to track down the broadside, but apparently no other copies had survived. At the university library, they told me that it was indeed a work printed around the year 1800, based on the quality of paper and the printing technology used. In bibliographies I found a mention that in 1801, the cathedral chapter of Turku had given the order to confiscate and destroy a broadside called *Joyful Song of King Gustaf*, which was filled with "pagan abominations". The author was unknown. I visited Turku briefly, but found nothing in the cathedral chapter archives that shed any light on the matter.

I did, however, discover something exciting in the Folklore Archives. There was no trace of the poem there either, but to pass the time I began investigating the documented folklore of Ikaalinen. Of "worm wind" and "Itch in the mouth of a fish" I found no mention. And, then, as closing time was approaching, an archivist brought me an uncatalogued binder labelled *Ikaalinen, Loimaa etc. 1885–1892.* I still had half an hour, enough time to leaf through this, though I did not expect to find anything. Suddenly, half way through the binder, *it* appeared: a yellowed sheet of paper with information collected by G. F. Rolfwén, year 1887. The source of the information was given as *Kopperskan Eva Mattsdotter i Ikalis, Ridiala by, 80 år. Hört från sin mormor såsom barn.* ("Folk healer Eva Mattsdotter in Ikaalinen, Riitiala village (this was in Ikaalinen), 80 years old. Heard from her grandmother as child.") Rolfwén had written down a number of old spells, some of which I already knew from elsewhere. Two of them, however, made my hands tremble:

To gain fisherman's luck.

A shoulder blade, or a piece of it, of a goat, preferably a white goat, is attached to a net on the first new moon after the breaking of the ice while reciting thrice:

> *Ies kuollut, äes kuollut,*
> *Aasa tuhti mullin mallin.*
> *Kutunluu ve'essä nukkuu,*
> *Satakuua maan sisässä.*

The Midnight Worm in Ikaalinen

("Yoke dead, harrow dead,
hefty *Aasa* in shambles.
Doe's bone [*kutunluu*] in water sleep,
Satakuua under the earth.")

There it was, that "*SATAKUUA under the earth*"!
The other spell was a defence against scabies,
burns, and fires:

> *Hus pois Kutka kalan suuhun,*
> *liekki syttyvä salassa.*
> *Mene poies Härjän päähän,*
> *nimettömän kokon kanssa*
> *siellä viettänet elosi.*

("Away with the Itch [*kutka*] to the mouth of
 a fish
a flame shall light in secret.
Away with you, to Bull's head,
with unnamed eagle,
there to live out your days.")

A complex rite of some sort was connected with this
spell, but the healer Eva could not remember it in its
entirety. A dried pike's head, a burning shingle, and
bull's horns were needed, but what magic was performed with them, even her grandmother could not
tell. However, here, finally, was irrefutable evidence
that Ikaalinen was home to previously unknown
folklore, of which Rolfwén was aware.

I later gave a talk on my findings at the licentiate
seminar of folkloristics, provoking a heated academic

51

argument. All of my interpretations were mercilessly torn to shreds, and, with hindsight, I must admit that this critique was entirely justified. The alternative interpretations were, however, no more convincing, the only interesting—and as I later found out, correct—hint coming from a participant who had studied the folklore of the German population of Transylvania. He cited this incomprehensible rote:

> *Astaroth, Sadok, Joch so tot,*
> *Zathucker kommt, wenn die Kristalle rot*

> ("Astaroth, Sadok, Yoke so dead,
> Zathucker comes, when the Crystal [is] red")

As he pointed out, the "yoke dead" from the third spell was also found here. *Aasa tuhti* might have been *Astaroth*. And it was within the realm of possibility that *Sadok* had become *Satakuua*. But what did it all mean? What was hidden behind these names? The seminar ended in mirth as the professor blurted out: "The unnamed eagle must, then, be Dracula."

In 1964, I wrote up my findings in a short research paper and published it in *Bibliophilos*, leaving out my wildest speculations. Thanks to this paper, I was soon put on the right track in my investigations, but just before that, I heard a story which deeply shocked me. Indeed, there was a terrible secret hidden on Ruutin-kari.

Chapter III

The Story of the Old Red Guardsman

In the autumn of 1964, I met an old labourer at the Tampere Railway station. We shall identify him as N, for his close relatives are still alive. We exchanged a few words about Ikaalinen, but then he said with some hesitation: "I have heard that the master has been asking about that old Rolfwén. I might tell you something. The wife always says I should tell somebody who understands. Such terrible things… But it will take some time. Is the master busy?"

The train was due to depart in a quarter of an hour, but, I had nothing urgent to do so I decided to take a later train. N did not wish to speak at the station, which was, he said, too crowded. On his suggestion, we took a trolleybus to Pispala and walked from there to the shore of lake Pyhäjärvi and back. N seemed to be on edge, frequently gazing over his shoulder to make sure that no eavesdroppers were following us.

He told me that in 1918 he had joined the Red Guard, as had many of his relatives. He was 17 years of age. One night he was sent to make an inspection in the house of master Rolfwén in Ruutinkari. Thus, I learned that Rolfwén's house had been built a few years before the First World War. Already at that time, Rolfwén was a well-known recluse, who did not

53

socialize with other people, but even given that, people wondered why he had chosen Ruutinkari. Merely transporting building materials there had been expensive. During the fortification works of the First World War people made fun of the fact by saying: "First old Rolfwén made his house on Ruutinkari, and now the emperor is doing the same."

The patrol arrived at nightfall and Rolfwén received them with mock courtesy ("Welcome to my humble abode," he said). To my question about the interior of that house of horrors N replied that it was very modestly furnished. There were only a couple of sparsely furnished rooms, but there were strange markings on the walls. "Many-pointed stars and such", as N described them. And in one corner on a small table there was a polished black stone, which *started to glow red* during their conversation.

I was startled when I remembered the words of that Transylvanian poem: *"Zathucker kommt, wenn die Kristalle rot."*

But N went on: The red guardsmen quickly inspected the house and found neither guns nor extra provisions. The leader of the patrol asked if the stone was, perhaps, a radio transmitter used to keep contact with the Whites. ("Nobody knew about those new gadgets then and there were some weird stories about them," explained N.) Rolfwén replied that the device was meant to measure earth rays, but it was not yet finished. When it was ready in about two weeks, he said, he would give it to use of the People's Commission for finding ores.

The Midnight Worm in Ikaalinen

The other guardsmen quickly found out that there was nothing remarkable in the cellar: some potatoes, vegetables, and salted fish, but not in such quantities that one could call it an illegal store of provisions.

"Well then, where are the guns?" the disappointed leader of the group barked.

"You should not care about guns. I have something more exciting to show you: my secret weapon, THE MIDNIGHT WORM!"

At that moment, Rolfwén lifted his head and shouted something incomprehensible. "It was not human speech. It was like the croaking of frogs and cawing of crows," N said.

Rolfwén's shout had hardly ended when a structure made of boards at the furthest wall of cellar collapsed and out burst a monster, the memory of which still caused N to shiver. From his halting account I learned that the monster resembled a three-metre-long black centipede with the claws of a crayfish and something akin to a distorted human head. ("It could not be a real animal. I have looked through *The Fauna of the World* many times, and all the animal books in the main Ikaalinen library, and in none of them is there a picture of a such a beast.")

The appearance of the monster was such a shock to N that he fled, howling. It is said that he was found in the wee hours in the Mänttikuja alley, raving incoherently. They had to take him to a mental hospital for a couple of weeks. ("Good thing it was that I was in the mad house then. The White Guards came to Ikaalinen and would have butchered me as well, I'm sure.")

N never again met his comrades. He was sure they had fallen to the monster. The details of the events were never investigated, for there was already much to do in the aftermath of the Civil War. It was widely believed that N's comrades had left for Tampere and died when the city was taken. But some dark shadow had fallen upon Rolfwén. Before, he had been deemed eccentric, but now the local people really dreaded him. It was as if they all knew that he was wrapped in the most caliginous secrets, though what they were was completely unknown.

"He had the beast for a few years," continued N, "because during the autumn slaughter they used to haul horrendous numbers of slaughtered animals to Ruutinkari: pigs, sheep, sometimes whole cow carcasses. Everybody wondered what he did with them, because the man was as thin as a skeleton and never had visitors. Somebody once asked him where all the meat was going and old Rolfwén said that he used it as crayfish bait. Crayfish bait, bullshit! Nobody ever used so much crayfish bait, and old Rolfwén didn't even catch crayfish very often. He was feeding the monster. I know it."

At some point in the early twenties, perhaps in 1920 itself, Rolfwén had apparently had enough of the monster. In a state of agitation he rowed to the market town, ordered bricks and cement, and demanded that they should be delivered immediately, no matter the cost. Nobody knew what he planned to do with these supplies, but N thought he had walled up the rear part of the cellar. Not long afterwards Rolfwén rented a cottage in Rantopää and brought all his possessions there. He seemed to be on the verge of mental collapse, an ashen-faced ruin of a man, talking to himself and paying no heed to others. ("Think on this: once at the gate of the market town he met the vicar's wife and the war councillor Sparfwén, but he didn't even notice them—he just continued mumbling to himself.") He spoke Swedish, so not much of it was comprehensible, but doctor Eränen, who had heard one of his monologues, claimed that it involved a *nameless cylinder* and *Leng plateau*, and *who the seals might break*. Doctor Eränen, who was also a correspondent for a local newspaper, was inspired to write a couple of articles about the malign effects of superstition.

Rolfwén did not have much time in his new home. By the following spring he had become completely deranged and had to be taken to Hatanpää, where he died a few years later. "He was calling for Satakuua and Kutunluu—a doe's bone—when they took him."

I hoped that the grim story of Rolfwén had finally come to the end, but soon discovered there was much more. On Ruutinkari there were snakes, and for this reason people dared not visit it. At the end of the twenties, two youths from out of town decided to land on the rock, oblivious to all warnings. Only one returned alive, shaking and afflicted with a deadly pallor. In the boat they found the body of his friend, swollen and blackened. The survivor explained that as they were approaching the island, he had felt an increasing uneasiness, which had finally turned into real dread. His comrade had also seemed anxious, but neither was willing to show cowardice to the other.

The Midnight Worm in Ikaalinen

They had barely landed when, as if by magic, a black snake, one and a half metres long, had appeared and bitten one of the young men. They rushed to the boat and started to row back, but death claimed the bite victim in a few minutes. The doctor was amazed by the case: adult men did not usually succumb to adder bites, or at least not so quickly. The death appeared to have been caused by some venomous tropical snake, but how could it survive the Finnish climate? And the continuation of the story was even queerer: the body was sent to the laboratory in Tampere for tests, but on the way there, *all the swelling disappeared.* Neither venom nor bite marks were found. The cause of death was recorded as a heart attack provoked by sudden shock.

It was not known if anybody had set foot on Ruutinkari since that incident. In the thirties, a group of adventurous boys went as far as planning a landing, but, as one of them later admitted, they couldn't summon the courage. When they were only a few metres from the shore, they became so afraid that they all agreed to turn back.

I thought that, now, the horrors had finally come to an end, but N continued his story. The summer before last, a terrible drowning accident had occurred on lake Kyrösjärvi: a motor boat had capsized and an entire family of three—mother, father, and their eight-year old daughter—had lost their lives. The bodies were never found. The accident was the cause of much speculation: the weather had been calm, nobody had consumed any alcohol, it could not have been a collision or a wreck, and all the family members were able to swim. In addition, N pointed out that the family's hunting dog had also been on the boat. Humans might drown, but one would expect the dog to be able to swim ashore. And, yet, not a trace of the animal had been found. On one autumn night, a cow had disappeared from pasture on a nearby island, and the rest of the herd had gone completely wild. And fishermen's nets had been torn quite often of late…

"Say what you will, but I believe that it's old Rolfwén's beast, the Midnight Worm, as he put it, that is on the loose again and rampaging about in Kyrösjärvi. *Can't anything be done about it?*"

N's story had filled me with trepidation. As far as I knew he was a sane, trustworthy man in control of his feelings, but, as the story progressed, he had become increasingly distraught. He spoke with a halting, trembling, and almost tearful voice and his last question had almost been a cry of anguish. What was to be done? What manner of beast could live for forty years walled up in a cellar?

I promised N that I would consider the matter and let him know as soon as I came up with a course of action.

I slept poorly the following night and with increasingly disturbing nightmares: gargantuan black centipedes chased me down the Pirulankuja lane. I fled to the nearest house, but the floor collapsed beneath me and I fell into a cave where grotesque creatures of many different shapes were moving around. Some resembled devils from folk tales, some were centipedes, while some—the most horrifying of all—had shapes that only a psychedelic artist could portray. Cacophonous music was playing in the background, occasionally interrupted when those present chanted: *Iä! Iä! Tsathoggua!* From the depths of the cave something black and horrible was approaching... I was aroused from sleep by the sound of my own scream and after drifting off again I dreamed that I was on board a green space ship that was actually *the nameless cylinder.* It was hurtling towards the plateau of Leng...

When, still trembling, I recollected my dreams in the morning... a thought came to me: *Tsathoggua— that was "Zathucker" and "Satakuua"!* Yes, but who or what was Tsathoggua? The only thing that came to mind was the state of Chad and the Ahaggar Mountains in the Sahara...

All morning I wrestled with the question of what to do with the abomination of the island of Ruutinkari. Should I turn to government officials I would be ridiculed. The morning post brought an unexpected solution to my conundrum. I received a letter complimenting my "fascinating article" in *Bibliophilo*s. It ended with a request to contact the sender, who was in possession of important additional facts. The sender was H. Herbert Bladh, *docent i kryptokronologi, Åbo Akademi* (included was a telephone number and address).

Chapter IV

The Scholar of Dark Secrets

A certain friend of mine, a resident of Turku, once told me that in his home city there was a saying: "Nobody knows what Bladh doesn't", which was a local adaptation of the Finnish saying about Plato. H. Herbert Bladh was a gentleman who was legendary for his erudition and enigmatic nature. His lectures covered a diverse range of subjects on the fringes of orthodox science. If there was indeed a person who could lead me to the right track, it was Bladh. I telephoned him right there and then, and managed to reach him. He seemed very excited and urged me to come that very day. When I began relating what I knew of Rolfwén, he became very serious and urged me to leave the topic for later. "We don't want to shock the eavesdroppers," he chuckled.

I arrived on a fast train to Turku Harbour and took a taxi from the station. Adjunct professor Bladh's residence was in a building the ground floor of which was occupied by the Department of Cryology of the Åbo Akademi University. On the first floor, one of the most extensive private libraries of our country was located. What little space was not claimed by bookshelves was shared by Bladh and his three cats: hoary Scua, fat, multi-coloured Feodora, and elegant, half-Persian Miranda. The gentleman himself was a small, portly, jovial person, comfortably dressed in a green silk robe ("in the Oblomov style," as he put it).

After welcoming me with a glass of port, my host got straight to business. On a table he had piled literature relating to the matter: massive scholarly folios, American paperbacks, and photocopies of manuscripts containing bizarre designs jostled for space. My host spoke at some length—one might say he gave a lecture of one and a half hours—but my attention never wavered.

I learned of a cluster of traditions called "the Cthulhu Mythos".

"Cthulhu or Cutulu, does that remind you of something?"

"*Kutunluu!*" I exclaimed spontaneously.

"Precisely. There you have an example of folk etymology: a foreign name is interpreted as a word conforming to one's own language. When the original meaning is lost, the domestic word is understood in a literal fashion and a belief system is built around it."

I recalled how Rolfwén had called out for Kutunluu and Satakuua when they came to take him to a mental institution. *He had been versed in that tradition...*

But Bladh continued his lecture. There were allusions to the Cthulhu Mythos in certain works which were difficult to locate, but hints could also be found in other texts, if one was able to interpret certain words correctly. The mythos was used in horror stories by the American writer Howard Phillips Lovecraft (1890–1937), whose followers continue to employ the same themes to this day. It was curious that Lovecraft should be so familiar with the subject, for he had certainly not read the majority of the works pertaining to the mythos. Initially he had regarded it as a pure product of the imagination, to be played with freely, but there were indications that, later, he had taken them very seriously indeed. And then he did die quite young...

Bladh's presentation was replete with barbaric names. He portrayed the Great Old Ones, of which Cthulhu was one. With vivid gestures he described R'lyeh, the cursed city sunken under the sea, with its "wrong geometry", as Lovecraft had put it. He conveyed the image of the Great Cthulhu, Lord of Horrors, who shall one day awaken and rise from R'lyeh; the blind imbecile Azathoth, who was "chaos, blasphemy, and madness at the centre of creation"; abhorrent faceless Nyarlathotep, howling in the night and storm, Hastur ("He whose name shall not be uttered", *Magnum Innominandum* as he was called in Latin manuscripts), banished to the Hyades star cluster. He described the attendants of the Great Old Ones, mythical Voorms, Dholes, Shoggoths and Tcho-Tcho people; he told me of vile, forbidden books, such as *The Spells of Dhole*s and *The Book of Eibon*; he explained underground rites and people who had summoned forbidden powers.

His words were so vivid that I nearly experienced those horrors for myself: the tentacles of the Great Cthulhu were reaching for my ankles; the giant bats of Hastur were speeding through space; I heard the screams of the scaly shantak birds and the croaking of the frog-headed Deep Ones, saw spheres of light gliding towards the ground, releasing black slime as they shattered...

"These spheres of light are connected to a certain Great Old One: Yog-Sothoth..."

"Yog-Sothoth—*Joch-so-tot!*" I cried out.

"Quite correct. There we find a German folk etymology, and when translated into Finnish it becomes *ies kuollut. Aasa tuhti* and Astaroth are of course Azathoth, and he is 'in shambles, *mullin mallin*', because chaos and madness are thought to be in Azathoth's nature. And the next Great Old One is the picean and formless Tsathoggua..."

"Tsathoggua!" I screamed, scrambling to my feet so that Miranda, who had curled next to me, left in indignation.

"Yes, Tsathoggua, or Sadogua in Latin, Sadok, Zathucker, Satakuua..."

With a trembling voice I described my previous night's dream to Bladh, and he listened, interested and nodding. "Your nightmare was quite right: according to the stories, Tsathoggua lives underground. I think that this is a case of Tsathoggua's cult. The servants of Tsathoggua were the dholes, also called the *Worms of Midnight.*"

"Good heavens, there is one loose in lake Kyrös-järvi," I cried. Then I took Bladh by the sleeve and told him in one great outpouring all I knew about Rolfwén, his black crystal and the Worm of Midnight, once again on the rampage. "By God, what must we do?" I finally asked.

Bladh had been pale and attentive as he listened to me. "There is no doubt that this is indeed a dhole

The Book of Poison

loose in Ikaalinen. We have to lay our plans very carefully. Never did I think I would come face to face with a dhole." Bladh's distress had passed and he assumed the appearance of a botanist delighted by the discovery of a new species. He suggested that we have tea as he arranged the pieces of this puzzle, before planning our action. I agreed, though I was impatient. Theoretical problems were of little interest to me.

Bladh continued his lecture, though with fewer words this time. He told me that *Kutka kalan suussa* —'Itch in the mouth of a fish'—was apparently a reference to the fire demon *Cthugha*, who resided in the star called Fomalhaut in the Southern Pisces constellation. Fomalhaut was Arabic for 'Mouth of the Fish'. The nameless eagle was clearly Hastur, whose abode was in the *Hyades* star cluster of the Taurus constellation. "Pnako-skills" was a reference to a book mentioned in the mythos, the *Pnakotic Manuscripts*: and verses pouring scorn over Reuterholm, "*Ei oo NECRO nyrkeissäsi, Apu allasi hajoa*", were apparently a reference to another forbidden book, the *Necronomicon*, and its supposed author, Abdul Alhazred the Arab. And, lastly, he came to a more practical question: "worm wind" did not involve wind at all. *Tuuli*, 'wind', was simply a distortion of the word *Dhole*.

"In a few seemingly incomprehensible folk poems we have the entire package of Cthulhu myths", Bladh explained in a satisfied manner while rubbing his hands together. He showed me the summary he had devised:

The Midnight Worm in Ikaalinen

CTHULHU MYTHOS	FINNISH	GERMAN
Tsathoggua or Sadogua	*Satakuua*	Zathucker, Sadok
Cthulhu	*Kutunluu* (Doe's bone)	—
Azathoth	*Aasa tuhti* (Hefty "*Aasa*")	Astaroth
Yog-Sothoth	*Ies kuollut* (Yoke dead)	Joch-so-tot
Hastur	*Nimetön kokko* (Un-named eagle)	—
Hyades	*Härän pää* (Bull's head)	—
Cthugha	*Kutka* (Itch)	—
Fomalhaut	*Kalan suu* (Mouth of a fish)	—
Pnacotic manuscripts	*Pnakotaidot* (Pnako-skills)	—
Necronomicon	NECRO	—
Abdul Alhazred	*Apu alla hajoaa* (Help crumbles beneath you)	—
Dhole	*Matotuuli* (Worm wind)	—

I had to admit that Bladh's solution to the enigma of the poems I had found was elegant. Truly, "Nobody knows what Bladh doesn't."

Then we started pondering the practical aspects of the problem. Bladh asked me to repeat my story, interjecting with very detailed questions as I talked; I couldn't fathom how some of his questions even related to the matter. He kept fetching books from his shelves, leafing through them, and mumbling "hm, hm." His notes filled a dozen pages. It was around two o'clock in the morning when he stopped.

"I will have to send a telegram to Cambridge and Göttingen tomorrow to obtain more information— and, of course, I should visit Ikaalinen to interview N—but the pattern appears to clarify."

"What are those dholes? How could such a creature live for forty years walled up in a cave?"

"Well, how should I put it?" They are not animals produced by our evolution. Their true abode is, as Lovecraft once said, "between dimensions". To put it another way, they hail from somewhere outside our three-dimensional universe. There is some truth behind the summoning rituals of those old books of witchcraft we ridicule as superstition. They describe —often in a misleading and naïve manner—acts which facilitate the arrival of dholes. The idea behind the incense and blood sacrifices is that, at first, the dholes take up some gaseous and liquid substances to build bodies for themselves. With time, they assume a more corporeal form and require increasing amounts of nourishment. Without it they wither, but are, nonetheless, incredibly resilient. The body of a dhole may be destroyed by fire or chemicals, but I do not know whether it dies or returns to its original habitat. The latter is supported in the old tradition by references to "sending them back to hell". I happen to own a classic in the field, the possession of which would be a source of pride for any university library— *sacrebleu!*"

"What is it?"

"What an idiot I am. I should have realized right at the beginning, when I heard about Göran Rolfwén... A moment please."

The Midnight Worm in Ikaalinen

Bladh picked up a quarto-sized book of about 200 pages from the table and showed it to me with some pride. It was *Die Dholen-Hexerey*—'The Witchcraft of the Dholes'—printed in Frankfurt in 1675.

"*The Witchcraft of the Dholes* is a real book after all. But take a look at the name of the previous owner."

Somebody had penned on the book's title page:

G. R.
1891

G. R.—Göran Rolfwén. Had he read this book on lonely nights in that accursed house on Ruutinkari? Was it there that he had embarked on his baneful quest and summoned the denizens of other worlds? Or had he succeeded earlier than that and merely taken himself to a place where he could live with his abhorrent companion, undisturbed by anybody? *Before old Rolfwén's time the worm wind blew from Matomäki.*

I asked Bladh for his opinion. He admitted that Matomäki may be an old, perhaps even prehistoric, cult site, where dholes had been summoned. Perhaps Rolfwén had found his own dhole there.

Bladh showed a clumsily drawn picture of a Worm of Midnight in the book. It matched N's description perfectly: a centipede with the claws of a crayfish or a scorpion and a vaguely humanoid head. The dhole in the picture was feasting on the entrails of a human it had just captured. From the size of the human, one could deduce that this dhole was at least ten metres in length.

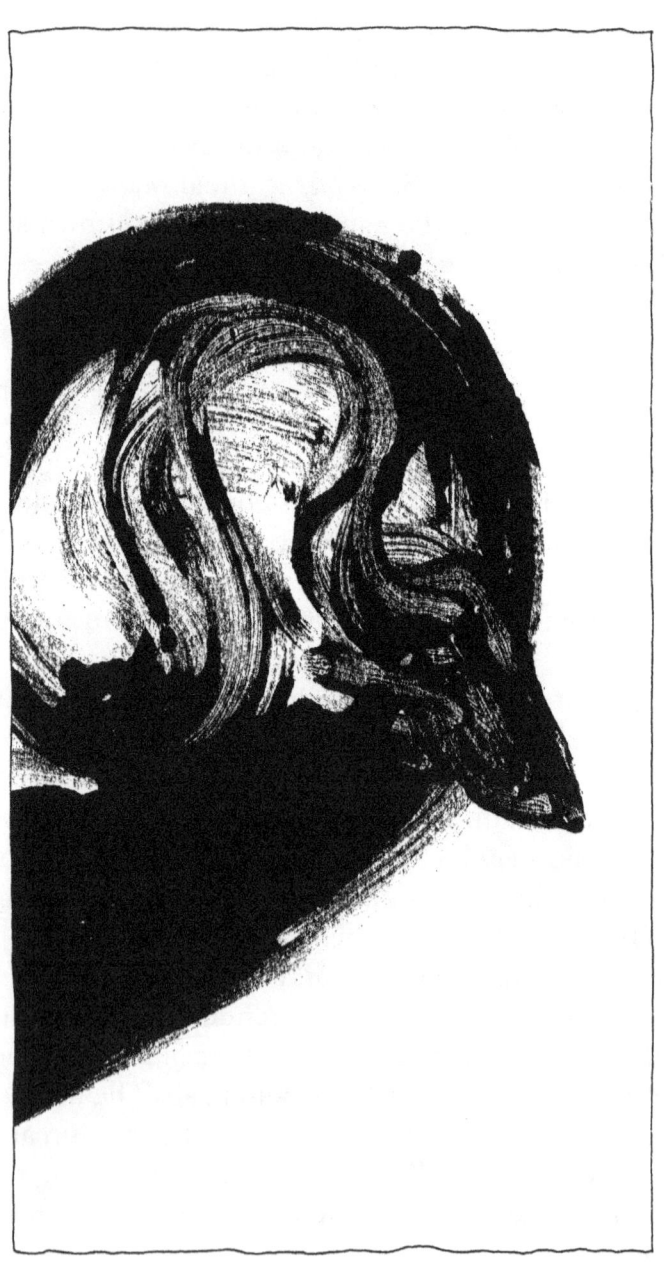

The Midnight Worm in Ikaalinen

I suddenly remembered somethings else and asked if the snakes on the island of Ruutinkari where perhaps also dholes.

"No, *mon ami*, that is quite another matter. It is interesting to note that Rolfwén was also versed in another forbidden tradition. A moment please—I have books related to that as well."

Bladh drew a few more works from his inexhaustible library and put them on the table. "This is perhaps the most interesting," he said, presenting an octavo of about fifty pages.

The title, in Latin, was, approximately, *Counsel of Tryphon Kelippos Hendekagrammatos on Drawing the Powers of the Stars into Talismans. Translated with Commentary by Clement Wardwell, Amsterdam 1685.*

Bladh explained that Tryphon Kelippos Hendekagrammatos was a fourteenth-century Byzantine monk. From his name one could deduce that he belonged to the order of Black Hendekagram, or elevenpointed star, with roots in Hellenic Alexandria.

I opened it at a random page and read out:

For this is a secret that the worshippers of the Twinned Snake Ftegel-Nets shall not know (and if they come to know it, let TRYPHON *strike them in his wrath): when your offspring has spent eleven times eleven days in the womb, when the Sun and Mars are in the first decan of Sagittarius and Saturn is ascendant, you shall lay the child on an altar for baptism…*

Bladh explained that the "child" referred to in the text was a black crystal, to be handled by revolting rituals of black magic, which at the end would be charged with psychic energy.

71

"Please do not ask me what psychic energy is. That, nobody could say. But it would appear that at the end of such rites a psychic electric fence, for lack of a better term, was sometimes created. The stone was surrounded by a circle, inside of which an uninitiated would receive telepathic impulses (mentioning a telepathic electric fence reminded me of the seagulls refusing to land on the island). The fact that anybody approaching Ruutinkari experienced great anxiety fits the theory perfectly. A telepathic radar would start operating when visitors were at a suitable distance. If they did not have the good sense to turn back in time, the next phase would be a telepathically induced hallucination. Now you understand how those snakes on Ruutinkari could survive the Finnish winter: *there were no snakes*. But the telepathic suggestion is so strong that a visitor will see a snake, feel its bite, and die from sheer shock. That crystal must still be there.

Chapter V

Two Visits to Ruutinkari

The following weeks were spent in curious pursuits. Frequently Bladh sent me on strange missions to Helsinki. Occasionally he wanted me to copy certain passages from the *Third Book of Steganography* by Trithemius or from the works of Arnaldus de Villanova. Sometimes I had to visit high-ranking officials

with a letter of recommendation from Bladh, asking
for certain permits, and then I had to check obscure
passages from the works of Clement Wardwell or
Caspar Unhold. We also visited Ikaalinen to get the
lay of the land. Bladh interviewed N and his wife
most carefully. At one point Bladh surprised me
thoroughly; he had asked N about Rolfwén's call, the
one which had summoned the dhole. "Was it like
this?" asked Bladh and uttered a sound impossible to
represent with letters. Something akin to this:

KRKPWP'FL N'GJA N'GJA UUAAGHH KRL KRL TSATHOGGUA FHTAGN! IÄ! TSATHOGGUA!

"Yeah, it sounded like that but, but old Rolfwén
yelled much louder," said N.

Bladh explained that he had spoken softly so as not
to disturb the peace of the neighbours or Ruutinkari.

After our preliminary investigations, we appeared in
Ikaalinen for a "winter holiday" in February 1965.
Bladh had acquired a set of skis from somewhere. He
was actually able to stay upright on them, even
though it was difficult to imagine him outside his
library. First, he visited the sheriff to show him
permissions signed by certain high-ranking officials
which stated that while conducting scientific experi-
ments we would have to perform an explosion or two
on Ruutinkari. As the island was uninhabited and the
detonations presented no danger to life or property,
the local public servants were requested to look

73

favourably on the project and lend assistance if needed.

Around noon we started our trek to Ruutinkari on our skis. One could clearly see that the place was avoided, for the pistes made a great bend around it. Before we left, Bladh had made sure I understood that the snake was merely a hallucination and posed no danger if one understood it as such and did not give in to panic. Furthermore, the "charge" on the black crystal had probably waned over the years, and thus it might be that we would see nothing. And, yet, I felt uneasy.

As we approached within a few metres of Ruutinkari shore I experienced for myself what I knew from the descriptions of other visitors: my mind was overcome by an unfathomable depression and a desire to abandon everything. As we continued, the depression gave way to a horror which I was barely able to contain. Once onshore we left our skis and ascended the icy rocks which required much care if one did not wish to sprain one's ankle. Then I heard the hiss... *I really saw* a black snake, though there was something tattered and insipid about it. As we walked towards the interior of the island, the snake floated continuously at my side, erect, and attacking.

"It's in quite bad shape, is it not?" said Bladh. "Concentrate your thoughts on the snake not having a head." I did as I was told, and the head of the snake vanished almost completely. The headless snake slid up the rock, staying at my side and making attacks, but it no longer felt threatening. However, my feeling of dread increased as we approached the house.

The Midnight Worm in Ikaalinen

Here it finally was: that house of horrors, abandoned for over forty years. From the outside it was nothing more than another abandoned, Finnish cottage, and even inside there was nothing to remind us of the former owner but a yellowed paper with a black eleven-pointed star and the letters *O.Q.* on the wall of the larger room. But, psychologically, it was almost impossible to step in: wave after wave of horror washed over me. At times even one step forward was too much to bear. I wanted to throw myself on the floor or to run away screaming, or *to strangle Bladh*. Had that accursed pretender hauled me here to perish? He was the cause of all the troubles. For a moment, I felt such wrath that I contemplated murder. I was startled when Bladh began to speak. His voice sounded as if it was coming to me from a great distance. The place apparently had an effect on him too, as he spoke haltingly and with a wavering voice: "Here we are, soon it will be over... we must find the place with the strongest feeling of hostility... be careful of the rotten floorboards."

It seemed to take an eternity to cover a distance of only a few metres in the room. Bladh had advised me to find the place with the strongest feeling of enmity. That would be the hiding place of the black crystal. Finally we found it: the northwestern corner of the larger room. On the floor were the remains of a carpet, which my friend removed. Underneath, the boards were loosely attached. Bladh took a hammer from his backpack and twisted three boards off. Of course, I should have offered my help, but I could not have taken a single step had my life depended on it. It took

75

all of my effort to maintain what little was left of my sanity. I saw the black stars of a forbidden space... shantaks shrieked around me... dholes crawled out of their caves. *Iä! Iä! Tsathoggua!* That frozen desert outside... were we not in forbidden Kadath? The black stone of the land of Mnar... the black stone. *Zathucker kommt, wenn die Kristalle rot...*

"*Ph'nglui mglw'nafh Cthulhu R'lyeh wgah'nagl fhtagn!*"

I woke up suddenly. Those words had been shouted by Bladh, and he, too, seemed to be on the verge of collapse. In his hands he held a rusty steel chest, which he then pushed out the window with extreme effort. Sweat ran down his face.

As the chest was cast out, the horror loosened its grip, but only slightly. Bladh said: "Well then, the second worst part is over."

"*Second* worst?"

"Yes, as I said, the crystal must be broken. And before that, we must open the chest. I shall open it, and, since you are younger and stronger, you will shatter the crystal." Bladh took a chisel from his backpack and went out. I followed, wondering if I would be able to perform my part of the task...

It seemed that Bladh laboured with the chest forever before he got it open. There it was, that black crystal, emanating the evil of all underground cults. I would not approach it, not for any price... and those snakes... the whole island was teeming with them.

"Seeing snakes?" asked Bladh in a voice meant to be cheerful, though it sounded more like the yelp of a wounded wolf. His words gave me a small measure of strength, and I was able to take the stone in my hand. It was about twenty centimetres long and ten centimetres wide at its widest point, a polished, irregular, crystal-like object with markings I did not understand on the surface. In reality, the stone did not weigh much, but lifting it felt almost impossible. I could barely raise it to the level of my chin. Limply, I threw the stone against a sharp projection in the bedrock.

As the stone hit the rock I saw a flash of green flame, and suddenly there were even more snakes. We would never escape with our lives, or at least not with our sanity. *Tibi, Magnum, Innominandum, signa stellarum nigrarum et Bufaniformis Sadoguae sigillum... Kutunluu ve'essä nukkuu, Satakuua maan sisässä...* soon He arrives...

•

Bladh shook me awake. I must say he used language that a drill sergeant would be ashamed of, but aggressive behaviour was needed to return me to any semblance of normality.

"A good start," said Bladh cheerfully. He pointed at the stone. A small piece had been chipped away. He took the chisel and the hammer, positioned the chisel on the break point and with all his strength hit it with the hammer.

Green flames engulfed the entire island. In the conflagration I could seesnakes and monsters for which there are no words in our language. There was an inhuman shriek that could be heard at the furthest reaches of lake Kyrösjärvi. The Earth shook under me and all the monstrosities of my nightmares came crawling out of their caves. *Iä! Tsathoggua!...*

The Midnight Worm in Ikaalinen

After a few minutes I returned to consciousness. Bladh told me that he, too, had fainted, but recovered just before me. He took a canteen from the backpack and took a mighty draught. The black stone lay next to him, broken in two pieces.

"So, it has been done, and we deserve a good tipple," said Bladh. He gave me the canteen. It contained cognac, and I took a large gulp myself. I felt exhaustion beyond measure.

"Do you think the green flame was seen very far away? I asked.

"Nonsense, it was a telepathic hallucination. Because the 'range' of that device is only a few dozen metres, nobody saw anything. And, now, there are a few routine matters to take care of."

We broke the black stone into small pieces; with the first strokes green flames still flashed around us and snakes could be seen, but as the stone broke into smaller and smaller pieces, these phenomena weakened and then ceased altogether. In the end we went in to see the place where we had found the chest. The cottage still felt hostile, but we didn't feel anything comparable to the previous horrors.

On the spot the chest had been discovered we found a collection of fist-sized, natural stones, positioned in the shape of the eleven-pointed star. We separated the stones and threw them out the window onto the ice. As the ice melted, the stones would sink to the bottom and no longer be harmful to anyone. But Bladh seemed to be missing something. He knocked on the walls, dug at the earth with the chisel, and finally pried away a floorboard (this time with my more effective help). And there it was, under the floor, a brittle, old goat's shoulder blade—*kutunluu*—marked with that ubiquitous eleven-pointed star which I did not recognize. Bladh explained that it marked the first decan of Sagittarius.

"Hm... I might try this for fisherman's luck," said Bladh, whose old mirth had returned. "It's a pity that we have to destroy interesting folkloristic material." He threw the shoulder blade on the floor and crushed it by stamping on it.

As we left, I glanced at my watch and noticed that we had only spent about half an hour on Ruutinkari, though it seemed that aeons had passed since our arrival. I tried to match Bladh's mood and asked (lifting my fur hat), if my hair had turned white. "Just barely grey," came the answer.

Once outside we checked the northern shore of the island. There was a cellar with a collapsed door and a gawping black hole in the rear wall. The previous horror started to sneak back into my mind. We had yet another task ahead of us... I was tired to the extreme, and asked Bladh if could postpone our expedition to another day.

"Not possible," answered Bladh. "It is aware of our deeds, though it will not venture out into the daylight. It is extremely dangerous to leave it free for even one night."

As we skied back we dropped the stone fragments into a hole in the ice left by an ice fisher. We also threw in the chest. Let them rest there till judgement day!

The Midnight Worm in Ikaalinen

I apologized to Bladh for proving so weak, but he dismissed my apology with a wave of his hand. "We both performed in a satisfactory manner, considering the circumstances," he said. "If one takes into consideration that we *knew* what to expect, what would have happened to people who did not? With that kind of system, physical strength and courage are of little use. The most important thing is not to give in to suggestion. And as I said, the powers of the stone were already waning. Forty years ago our knowledge and fortitude would have been of no avail."

"How is it possible that goods were delivered to Rolfwén from time to time, as we have heard?"

"Well, the system is somewhat like a radar. When he was expecting something, he turned off the power, so to speak."

We returned to the hotel, where we had the opportunity to sleep for a few hours before continuing our labours. N had left us a message: in the envelope was a photograph of Rolfwén from the year 1895, cut from a local newspaper. In the picture was a tall and gaunt youth, serious looking with a thin face, a high forehead, and a long chin. There he was, an enemy whose abilities we had reluctantly come to appreciate.

The sun was setting as we prepared for our second expedition. Bladh opened a small trunk, which he had handled with great care during our entire trip. I was quite shocked to see it contained dynamite. We carried the trunk out very carefully and placed it on a sledge Bladh had rented. Getting onto the ice with the sledge was not simple: to avoid a long detour through Kiviniemi, we had to take the risk of riding it down a steep slope. Bladh, as always avoiding arduous work, chose the shortest and steepest route. From the hotel to the shore of Kyrösjärvi ran a road called Tenkooli, and we rode down it with the sledge. Bladh sat in the back, holding the trunk and the skis, and I steered to the best of my ability. As we reached the lake we sighed in relief, put on the skis, and started hauling the sledge. The sun had already set, and by the time we reached Ruutinkari, it was already dark. What little light there was came from the stars. As the black crystal was gone, no snakes were in sight, but the other kind of horror was almost as strong. There, behind the cellar door which loomed before us, hid the monster of bygone aeons, the Worm of Midnight, which for such a long time had stalked Ikaalinen. I thought I heard something slouching upwards as we ascended the rocks…

On the rock, Bladh sounded with all his might that inhuman call, which had already shocked me when delivered in a quiet voice. We heard sounds from the cellar, and, surrounded by eerie phosphorescence, the monster appeared. There it was, that abomination from another dimension, the Worm of Night, servant of the black and formless Tsathoggua, the one who demands bloody sacrifices and the object of ritual subterranean worship!

We threw our explosives into the cellar and took cover. The explosion left us deaf for several minutes, rocky fragments rained down upon us, and the sounds echoed from shore to shore. In place of a cellar there was now a pile of rubble emitting fetid smoke. The chimney and the north wall of the house had succumbed to the power of the detonation (in the spring the house was demolished and the remains were taken to Kasinonranta shore to be burned in a midsummer bonfire).

Of how we returned to the hotel and took a taxi to Tampere, I have very little recollection. It was erased from myj mind by a singular image, which still occasionally haunts me in my sleep: *the face of that Worm of Midnight was the face of Göran Rolfwén, distorted by hatred and emanating malevolence. As we prepared to throw the dynamite he cried in a hissing inhuman voice: "I shall return!" For the Worm of Night is undying, and the signs of forbidden stars shall summon him upon Earth, and behind the dholes arrives He, the horror of countless aeons, black and formless Tsathoggua!*

—Translated from the Finnish by Tino Warinowski

Paappana

or

Erkki Santanen's Music

A good while back, there was a lot of talk in our city about Paappana as an unrivalled meeting place for young people. It was the music that drew them there, of course, live music that sprung from the youngsters' own fingers, from their electric guitars and basses, their synthesisers and drum kits.

All manner of young people would make the pilgrimage to Paappana. Wherever you would bump into a couple of teenagers, you'd hear them recounting some adventure about Paappana, about the excellent band that was playing there at the last concert or at some improvised session. And no one had a bad word to say about the bands. "I heard 'The Outlaws of Destiny' playing in Paappana, and believe me, they've changed a lot since I last heard them. Make is really something on the guitar, and you should hear Kake's drum solo. What rhythms! You'd think he had at least four hands. And wait till I tell you about the best bit: Jokke learned to sing—he has a voice that would put others to shame now!"

Paappana, or Erkki Santanen's Music

That's the sort of thing the people who went to Paappana would be saying. There was some extraordinary magic about the place, at least where music was concerned. Paappana made maestros out of the most mediocre of singers, and those who were only capable of strumming a couple of notes on the bass—and who were only playing at all to do a favour for a mate—would realize that they could play after all, and that they really wanted to learn more.

It was widely believed that rock music and drugs were synonymous, but if you went to Paappana, you'd see that they weren't, not there. The motto of the place was that music was the strongest drug around. Anyone who was keen on the drink or on marijuana would throw away their bottle or their joint when they heard the sweet music in that place.

Now, you would associate sex with that kind of singing too. And indeed, if you were looking for love, you'd be as well to head for Paappana. There every heart was happy, and the most beautiful girls would respond kindly to the wooing of even the shyest boys. The most unlikely of couples were formed in Paappana. Even a disco queen could fall in love with a bookworm, or a leather-clad hunk with a quiet girl with glasses like milk-bottle bottoms. And it was a love that would last long after the first encounter, although no one would have expected it.

That's the kind of place Paappana was, the rock-music club in an old factory building. Actually, Paappana was the name of the whole suburb, but in the eyes of those who lived in the rest of the city, Paappana was synonymous with the factory. No one lived in the damp, rotten housing in the area itself, except for petty criminals and beggars, backstreet winos and unemployed people, and people certainly didn't come to visit them. There were also a few nice, mild-mannered old people there, pensioners who couldn't afford to leave the area. When a musicians' club started up in the former factory, these people were standoffish with the newcomers and suspicious of them, worried that junkies would soon be following on the singers' heels—it was ironic that they should be so concerned about that, given how fond of drinking most of the inhabitants of the suburb were. But music is a good mediator, and after they had had a listen themselves to what the clubbers were doing, most of the local people came to the conclusion that it was great to see enthusiastic young people around livening the place up a bit.

The club was overflowing with top-class musicians, but nevertheless, there was one person who excelled over and above the rest of them. Erkki was his name, Erkki Santanen. He was a lively young man, and music was the guiding star of his life, but at the same time he was good company and was always willing to lend an ear to others, to find out whether they felt the same passion for anything in life as he did for music. If they did, he would happily let them talk about it and listen attentively. If they didn't, he would do his best to explain to them why it was so important to have a cause and a goal to keep you going. That's the kind of man Erkki Santanen was, when he was still on top form. Though he was interested in music, he was interested in people as well, and at the end of the day, it amounted to the same thing.

When the life and music of Paappana were at their height, it was Erkki Santanen who best embodied the spirit of the club. But as time passed, life in the place started getting out of order, just as Erkki himself lost his way. I know what you're thinking, but it wasn't like that. There were no drugs or drunkenness involved. He just lost interest in companionship and friendship. His eyes began to shine strangely and his voice took on a fanatical edge. He was striving for a new kind of music, a perfection like no other in the world, and instead of jamming with other musicians, he started skulking about by himself down in the basement and pottering with his synthesizer to compose his music.

And the people who got to listen to what Erkki was up to now were all left terrified and shaken. One of them lost his mind completely and eventually killed himself after spending two months in a lunatic asylum. Erkki didn't give a damn about that, though, as he was so caught up in his music that he didn't bother about other people anymore—it made no difference to him if they were alive or dead.

It was completely unearthly music. Very few people heard it, since most of Erkki's old friends lost all contact with him as he closed up in himself more and more. Even so, some people were allowed in, and those who were willing to talk about what they had heard said that there were rhythms that didn't keep time even with themselves, and when you listened to the music all sorts of strange thoughts would run through your head, just as if you were under the influence of psychedelic drugs. You would see colours your eyes had never seen before, you would get glimpses of foreign lands and cities under strange skies, on other planets, and you would see strange, otherworldly monsters on the streets of those cities.

That was what Erkki Santanen's music was like, music that certainly did nothing for your sanity. And in the end it was this music that was the Paappana club's downfall. For Erkki had become so quiet, so taciturn, so aloof, so strange in his ways that people were starting to worry about him. As Erkki withdrew further and further into his own little world, the old spirit abandoned the place. The musicians were gloomy now, and it showed in their music. They went looking for a place to jam in other suburbs, and people stopped coming to see and listen to them. In the end, the place was left to Erkki, Erkki Santanen who had become such an oddball, whose thick beard hadn't seen a razor for a long time, nor his wild mane of hair a comb. To look at him, you would think he was a madman, or a caveman from the Stone Age, or both.

Then, Erkki went missing. What friends he still had didn't report it to the police at first, for as you might imagine, someone like him would often disappear for a while, in search of charity or inspiration, but he would always come back in the end. But now nobody had the faintest idea where he was. He hadn't been seen in his usual haunts, and when anyone who knew him went to Paappana, they saw that his instruments were there gathering dust. It was a bad sign. Although the man had gone completely astray, it was still really important to him to keep his instruments in good repair and in order and clean. To tell the truth, now that music had become his sole purpose in life, he was looking after the tools of his trade even more carefully than ever, even though his very person was taking on a rather Neanderthalesque look.

The police turned the old factory upside down looking for him, and then they combed the whole area, but they never found the young man or his body. They knew of a couple of men living in the area who had committed serious crimes in their youth and spent a long time in prison. They cross-examined these men harshly, but they couldn't help the police with their enquiries either. In fact they swore that it would never occur to them to harm any of the young musicians. They were as sorry as anyone about the way the music had forsaken the area, and were really pleased with what the young musicians were doing, while it lasted. The officer in charge of the investigation was of the opinion that the former criminals were being honest about their lack of involvement in Erkki's disappearance, and so he let them go as soon as he had taken their statements.

Year after year went by and the golden days of the old factory were forgotten. Or were they? Perhaps they weren't forgotten after all. The couples who had fallen in love in Paappana got married, most of them at least. They couldn't forsake their memories of the place, for well they knew that their big day would never have come about were it not for the musicians' club in Paappana, once upon a time. At the same time, they knew that there was something odd in that old factory building. The local people avoided it, though you would think at least some of them would be eager to hear those musicians who still played there. The building had large windows, as do most old red-brick factories, and anyone passing by could see Erkki Santanen's musical instruments inside. Why didn't anyone steal them, since the young man who owned them had been missing for several years now? But even though their owner had gone, it seemed that the musical instruments had no intention of going anywhere. People were reluctant to go in or interfere with his things. Did they think there was some kind of curse on them?

The situation was so strange that a group of young men who knew each other since the Paappana days started getting together regularly to share their memories of the club and—gradually—to plan reconnaissance trips. The head of the group was a young historian called Robert Bladh. He had just graduated from university, but what's more, he had an uncle—or great uncle, perhaps—who had died a couple of years earlier, an old man by the name of Herbert Bladh, who had left behind a whole archive of documents and notes about the occult. And Robert was of the opinion that those documents might be helpful to whoever decided to investigate the mysteries of Paappana.

The occult, you say? You might think that was just something to amuse old crones. But you'd be wrong. While he was rummaging through his uncle's documents, Robert came across evidence that the old man had taken a mysterious trip to Ikaalinen, a small city in the west of the country, to lay some kind of spectre. The story was that a man named Göran Rolfwén—a learned man who was into the occult and mysticism—had summoned some sort of unearthly serpent to life to do his bidding. He wasn't able to control the monster, though, and as the story turned out, the beast got completely out of hand and escaped to settle in Kyrösjärvi, the beautiful lake near Ikaalinen. The monster spent decades running amok in the lake and causing trouble. It might kill a cow that was grazing in the meadow next to the lake, for example, or snatch little toddlers from the shore. Sometimes it would attack the boats crossing the lake. Since the local people were unable to make head nor tail of these attacks, they couldn't put a stop to them either. But Herbert Bladh didn't waste any time in acting when he promised a young learned man from Ikaalinen that he would banish the worm from this universe back to the dimension betwixt and between whence it had originally come.

When Robert started going on about this, the other people from the group at first jumped to the conclusion that the poor man was losing his mind. But he was as level-headed as ever though, and had never been one for superstition. He had been a computer geek when he was young, and had a very scientific worldview that denied any kind of supernatural element. When he went to Paappana, he met Tanja-petra Janatuinen, a good-looking girl whose only interests seemed to be nice clothes and her own appearance, although she was doing reasonably well in school. Paappana worked its usual magic and made

91

a couple out of them, and the pair of them changed under each other's influence and eventually went to study history together. Now, Tanjapetra was teaching at a school in the city and Robert was writing his PhD thesis.

On the whole, Robert was someone who wouldn't yield to superstition: he had been a man of reason and science since he was young. As well as that, he was settling down as a married man now. There was every chance that he'd have a family of his own in a couple of years' time. So, after the initial shock, his friends were happy to listen to what he had to say.

Robert said that his uncle Herbert had gathered a wealth of information about supernatural activity, and was able to explain most of it scientifically. Well, sort of scientifically, you could say. Herbert would have to have recourse to scientific concepts that weren't widely accepted. Nonetheless, Robert was of the opinion that it wouldn't be impossible to reconcile these concepts with modern physics. In any case, the conclusion that Robert drew from his uncle's work was that the old man had worked out the natural laws of the "dimensions betwixt and between", so that there was a system or theory coming together. Robert believed these laws could be learnt and the relationship between them understood by studying the notes the old fellow had made in his day, and he put together the most important bits of the material for his friends, so that they could draw their own conclusions from his uncle's theories.

As well as that, Robert got in touch with the man who had taken Herbert around on a tour of Ikaalinen forty-odd years before. By now the man was grey and balding, but on the other hand, he was a university professor and a renowned philosopher now. The Professor sent his sincerest apologies at first, but in the end he agreed to come and visit the circle of young men to recount the story of the trip to them, since Robert thought it best that his companions be aware of the details of the expedition, in case they visited the old factory and found something odd or frightening there.

Tanjapetra could see that her husband was up to something unusual with his friends. At first she tried to make little of the whole affair, but as the weeks drew on her patience started to fail, and in the end she decided to ask Robert the fateful question. And of course, the man could hardly send his own wife away with an excuse. At the end of the day, it was the club in the old factory in Paappana where they had met and fallen in love. So Tanjapetra had a right to know the truth, however unpalatable it might be.

And Robert told her everything: that he and the other members of the group were curious about the old factory and wanted to reveal the secret of Paappana, if there was one, or at least to understand it. Tanjapetra remained in silence for a while, mulling over what her husband had said. On the one hand, she would have preferred to forget about Paappana and enjoy the nice life she and Robert, still head over heels in love with each other, were living in the present. On the other hand, she could well understand why her husband was interested in doing this. The spell Paappana had cast on her as a teenager, the otherworldly atmosphere that earned the club its reputation in the first place; it was something that had stuck in Tanjapetra's memory, something that went to the very core of her being. In a way, life had seemed insipid to her after the Paappana days, except for the fact that she had married a man who had once felt that same magic.

If Robert were happy not to go nosing around the old factory, he wouldn't be the man Tanjapetra married. It was as simple as that. She needed a man whose life had been changed by Paappana, and the price she had to pay for that was that the man would be curious about how his life had been changed, about the forces behind it.

So Tanjapetra said to her husband: "I'd prefer you to be here, rather than out there trying to coax monsters out of the old factory. I don't even know if the old ruin is still standing at all. But I suppose you can't help but satisfy your curiosity, and in a way I understand you. After all, it was the Paappana club that brought us together, wasn't it?"

Robert was overjoyed that his wife was so understanding, but in fact he hadn't expected anything less of her. As for her, she wanted to find out whether there was any supernatural explanation for the magic that Paappana had worked for a while and how the atmosphere had gone to the dogs afterwards. She was an old-fashioned woman too, a woman who preferred to leave such a scary mission to her husband, and who could blame her for that? But even so, her conscience was pricking her. Perhaps, when it came to the crunch, she should stop her husband from having anything to do with Paappana. Perhaps she should go to see Paappana together with him and his friends. But her heart wouldn't let her do any such thing, though she hated to think of her husband out there while she was safe at home…

She tried to make light of these misgivings. For goodness sake, it was only an old factory in a suburb just a couple of miles from the city centre, but she was worrying about her husband as if he were preparing for an expedition to the South Pole! Wouldn't it be better for her to let Robert do what he wants—he wasn't going to find the slightest thing out of the ordinary there, and the biggest danger would be that that old ruin would fall down on top of him!

But, on the other hand, that in itself was a danger she couldn't ignore…

Tanjapetra sighed. She wished the men had already gone on their expedition and Robert was telling her about it at the kitchen table. Of course, there would be no monsters there at all. Robert would come home again and describe in great detail what was left of the old factory. They would get a chance to go back down memory lane to the Paappana days when the club was in its heyday, and her and Robert just getting to know each other well…

One day, when spring was brushing aside the last remnants of snow, the men set off for Paappana, the suburb none of them had been to for at least six years. As for the women—the girls they had met in Paappana as teenagers—they all stayed at home, some of them worried, like Tanjapetra, the rest of them joking about "the boys' spring picnic". "Men have always had their masonic lodges," one of them, a girl named Piiajonna, said to Tanjapetra with a mocking laugh. Tanjapetra tried to force out a chuckle herself but, despite her efforts, all she could feel was her heart sinking deeper into her, and a shiver went down her spine as if she was perishing with cold. It was strange how Piiajonna had changed since her school days, the days of Paappana, thought Tanjapetra. When they were teenagers, Piiajonna was the quiet, pious girl who would not put up with bawdiness, while Tanjapetra would be making a right show of herself and shocking people with her swearing and her forthrightness in talking about sex. Now, Piiajonna was the foulmouthed one who was all talk, and Tanjapetra wouldn't dream of acting like that any more. To tell the truth, when she watched some of the videos that were still around from those days, she was ashamed to admit that that rascal of a girl was her. There it is again—the magic of the old factory! The people who had gone to Paappana during the club's golden days had all changed radically because of the atmosphere in that place.

Though Paappana was a poor area when the club was up and running, it had gone completely to the bad in the intervening years, or that was what everyone said in the city centre, at least. There were only a couple of buses a day that went that way, since there was no need for any more. There was only a handful of people left living there, and even the alcoholics had abandoned the old houses, those of them who weren't already pushing up daisies. It was all over the papers a year or two ago that druggies were squatting in some derelict building there—not in the old factory, but some wooden house that the rot had been eating away at for ages—and that the police had had to use force to dislodge the addicts. They were the only ones who were heading for Paappana of their own accord these days, while everyone else was busy trying to get away from that backwater.

The only company Robert and his friends had on the bus there was an old man. He was a kind, talkative and companionable old fellow, though, and when he saw these well-dressed young men going to Paappana, he took an interest in them and struck up a conversation. When he learned that the group was going to Paappana to take a look at the old factory, his tongue loosened right away, for he himself was nostalgic for the good old days of music, the final flowering of Paappana.

"Oh, the musicians' club," he said, "I remember it well! Singers would be coming to Paappana day after day, with all the young people hot on their heels. Great times they were, great times! Young folk enjoying life to the full, but, believe it or not, we never had any trouble from any of them. Or with any of you, I should say," he smiled. "Though of course, there were young couples, boys and girls kissing and hugging each other. You would have to be careful not to trip over them! The area was alive with them in those days! You lads must have had plenty of girls yourselves when the Paappana club was in its prime!"

The young men liked the old fellow and were happy to admit that every single one of them had met his future wife in Paappana. The old boy burst out laughing and congratulated the young men on their good fortune. Then they started asking him about what kind of state Paappana—both the suburb and the club—was in these days, and their travelling companion's expression suddenly changed. Well, he said, however bad a state Paappana was in back then, the area was much worse today. He himself wouldn't go near the place if it weren't for the fact that an old friend of his was living there, a man who couldn't afford to live in any other part of the city. His friend was even older than him, and he would go and help him out and look after him from time to time, since he himself was still mobile enough.

As for the old factory, it was indeed still standing, but the local people were reluctant to go anywhere near it. "It's strange," said the old man pensively, "one afternoon a couple of years ago, when my friend was still able to go for walks, we were talking about when the young musicians were around and we decided to take a stroll and go and see the old club, for old time's sake. When we got face to face with the old building, we were reluctant to get any closer. We weren't tired at all, and in those days my friend was as hale and sprightly as me, but even so, we felt an aversion towards the factory. To be honest, you could say that we were sort of scared too. Anyhow, we turned back and neither of us went down to the factory again. And we've heard that many other people around here took fright in the same way when they went near the factory. People generally avoid the place."

But this man was proud of the fact that he wasn't superstitious. When Robert asked him whether he

thought supernatural forces of some kind were at work in the ruins of the old factory, he denied it outright and said he was ashamed of having been frightened in that way. He said he hoped Robert and these young men, if they were so interested in the factory building, would search the building and its contents for themselves. The old man didn't think the police had done their job well enough when they were looking for Erkki Santanen all those years ago. "If people give credit to the horror stories that are told about Paappana," the old man explained to Robert and his friends, "the reason is that no one knows what happened to that poor lad."

When the bus reached the stop in Paappana, the old fellow bade the young men a hearty farewell, and urged them to "do a good job". Robert and the lads were well pleased with how their expedition had begun, and all had a good word to say about how warm their welcome had been. They really had resolved to "do a good job". Of course, they were a little apprehensive about what they might see in the factory building. There was every chance that they might come across the bare bones of Erkki Santanen there, if the man on the bus was right that the police weren't doing their job properly. But what if they did find his skeleton? It's living people who are the murderers. As for Erkki Santanen himself, although he had become a bit cantankerous in the end, he was a nice guy in his day, and Robert didn't believe that he would change his ways once he died.

Then, the men set off in the direction of the old factory. They knew well how to get there, and as they headed down the road in the direction of the building they started to talk amongst themselves and, unsurprisingly, the conversation turned to the days of the club. But, just as the old man had said, there was a strange invisible wall around the building. When Robert and his followers saw the factory ahead of them, they felt a sudden reluctance. What the hell were they doing here? Wouldn't it be better to be tucked up at home with your wife, watching *Hill Street Blues* on that channel that shows all the old series?

Then, Robert broke the silence. "If we all got the same feeling at the same time, it's a false emotion. There's some device in there that's sending us away. Let's carry on until we find out what's in there."

He kept going in the direction of the factory. When the others saw that he was able to conquer his fear, they came after him as far as the building.

"How are you feeling?" he asked the rest of them. "Does anyone feel light-headed or heavy-hearted?"

None of the group felt that bad. "OK," said Robert. "My uncle said in his writings that you could see imaginary snakes around the old house where the monster was in hiding, and that the suggestion was so strong that one or two people died from a heart attack when they thought a snake bit them. Whatever device there is here, it seems it isn't able to perform that kind of suggestion on us."

"Do you think we should find that device—that we should break it?" one of the men asked.

"Well, not yet. If there's something dangerous in there, some monster we're not able to contain, it's best to leave this place 'closed off', for public safety.

Paappana, or Erkki Santanen's Music

It's better if people don't come here and unleash that danger on themselves."

You would think that these words might startle the men, but the false fear caused by the building was troubling them even more. It was difficult to keep that fear under control, and it kept on growing the closer they got to the main entrance. Robert opened the door and crossed the threshold. When he found himself within the confines of the building, his fear vanished completely. And it was the same for the rest of them. They were all taken aback at how comfortable they felt in there.

The place had changed little from how they remembered it. To tell the truth, there wasn't nearly as much dust as they had imagined there would be. Erkki Santanen's musical instruments were lying there in the usual place, and looking reasonably well. If you wanted to play a bit of music, you would have to clean them, but then, all you would need to do would be to plug them in... But was there electricity? Yes, it seemed so. "The Council pays for it," said one of the men. He worked for the Council and had got permission for the group of friends to visit the place. "It's Council policy to keep the lighting on in abandoned buildings like this. If we go down to the basement, we can turn on the lights down there. We won't have to rely just on electric torches."

"What do you make of the air in here?" said Robert suddenly. "You'd think we'd be smothered by the dust, but we're not. As well as that, there's a bit of a draught in here, as if there was a ventilator, but I don't hear the sound of any machine. And don't you think it smells like a cellar here?"

The rest of them agreed with him. The draught was coming up from the basement. They decided, against their better judgement, to go downstairs and search the basement, which they did without further ado. Down there they turned on the lights, or the bare light bulbs that were hanging from the ceiling by electric cables, and spent a while staring at the bare white walls.

Then, the Council worker let out a small shriek. When the rest of them turned around to see what was wrong, he was white with fear and was pointing with his right hand. When the rest of them looked where he was pointing, they saw that the stairs continued down to another floor below the basement. Two underground storeys? No one was expecting that. None of them remembered from the club days that there had been a second basement.

The draught was stronger down here, and the men could feel it blowing up through the stairwell from below. It was cold, a strange cold that would penetrate to your very core—a cold that was much more frightful and piercing than normal freezing cold, a cold unknown to thermometers.

And when they descended to the floor below the basement, they began to understand. The layout of this floor was like the basement, but there was no lighting, not even bare bulbs. There was no need for it, for there was a cold blue light emanating from the far wall. The whole wall was glowing with this light, and when they went up to the wall they realized that

it wasn't in fact a wall, but a curtain, undulating in the slight breeze.

Robert drew the curtain aside, and when the men saw what was on the other side revealing itself before their eyes, they realized that this was where Erkki Santanen had got the inspiration for the new sort of music he was trying to compose.

There was a sort of space, a sky, or another universe, all ablaze with the blue glow. In front of this backdrop, however, the men could see celestial bodies or planets floating about in the void and giving off different colours, like a rainbow. These planets were crossing the sky slowly and majestically. Sometimes, two of them would pass so close to each other that you'd think they would collide. But they didn't, all that would happen is that one planet would gently engulf the other, leaving a single planet, larger than either of the two that had previously existed. And as their eyes got accustomed to this wondrous sight, the men heard a new kind of music, music that enchanted each and every one of them. That was Erkki Santanen's music, or the kind of music Erkki wanted to recreate with his instruments. And when this music caught hold of their minds, it would never loosen its grip.

One by one the men crossed over, leaving the room below the basement behind them to go and float away into the blue space. They had no choice anyway. For when the man from the Council looked over his shoulder, he saw that the stairs had disappeared.

—Translated from the Irish by Colin Parmar

www.ingramcontent.com/pod-product-compliance
Lightning Source LLC
Chambersburg PA
CBHW020629250626
47154CB00004B/1740